"I told Lynne three songs," Dana said. "I really should get back to the band."

Prince Arthur's arms remained around Dana for a moment longer. At last he released her, but with obvious reluctance. "Thank you for the dance."

"I . . . I enjoyed it," Dana murmured.

They stepped apart, still staring deep into each other's eyes. Finally, Dana tore her gaze from Arthur's and returned to her place in front of the microphone.

She checked the playlist, then began belting out "Late Last Night," one of her favorite songs. As she sang, she felt euphoric, as if she were floating above the ground.

She hadn't felt this way since . . . since the last time she fell in love, Dana realized with a shock.

Something terrible was happening to her, something terrible—and wonderful.

Arthur Castillo stands for something I despise, she reminded herself. But it didn't matter. She was falling in love with him anyway.

Bantam Books in the Sweet Valley High series
Ask your bookseller for the books you have missed

IN LOVE
WITH A PRINCE

Written by
Kate William

Created by
FRANCINE PASCAL

BANTAM BOOKS
NEW YORK • TORONTO • LONDON • SYDNEY • AUCKLAND

RL 6, IL age 12 and up

IN LOVE WITH A PRINCE
A Bantam Book / February 1993

Produced by Daniel Weiss Associates, Inc.
33 West 17th Street
New York, NY 10011

Cover art by James Mathewuse

ISBN 0-553-29237-4

Published simultaneously in the United States and Canada

PRINTED IN THE UNITED STATES OF AMERICA

OPM   0 9 8 7 6 5 4 3 2 1

IN LOVE
WITH A PRINCE

One

"Just one more day and he'll be here!" sixteen-year-old Jessica Wakefield announced as she deposited her tray at the crowded lunch table on Friday.

"Arthur Castillo, crown prince of Santa Dora," Lila Fowler said dreamily. "The richest, handsomest boy in the world."

"I still have so much to do to get ready!" exclaimed Amy Sutton. "I need a haircut, and a manicure, and *what* am I going to wear to school on Monday?"

The boys at the table—Todd Wilkins, Barry Rork, Ken Matthews, and Winston Egbert—did not seem to appreciate this turn in the conversation.

"I don't think we need to dress up for Arthur," Elizabeth Wakefield remarked, the corners of her blue-green eyes crinkling with amusement. "He probably wouldn't even notice—remember, he's just an ordinary guy."

1

"Just an ordinary guy." Jessica shook her head. How could her twin sister be so naive? "By definition, Liz, a prince can't be an ordinary guy. Besides, it's been five years since Arthur came to Sweet Valley as an exchange student. I bet these days he notices the way a girl dresses."

Jessica reached into her book bag and pulled out a copy of a tabloid newspaper. Prince Arthur's picture was splashed across the front page. "See? Here he is in London a few weeks ago with Princess Diana. Arthur's used to hanging out with the most glamorous people in the world!"

Elizabeth smiled. There was no point in arguing; nothing would stop Jessica from viewing Prince Arthur's upcoming visit as the event of the century. *And admit it*, Elizabeth said to herself, sneaking a peek at the tabloid story, *you're as excited as she is!*

Twins Jessica and Elizabeth *looked* exactly alike. Both were slim, blond, and suntanned, the epitome of classic southern California beauty. But they tended to *think* differently about most things. Elizabeth, older by four minutes, was considered the more serious twin. She was a model student and wanted to be a professional writer someday. With that goal in mind, she spent hours each week researching and writing articles for the Sweet Valley High newspaper, *The Oracle*. In her free time, she enjoyed quiet pursuits: a walk on the beach with her boyfriend, Todd Wilkins, a long talk with her best friend, Enid Rollins, or an hour alone writing in her journal. Jessica, on the other hand, thrived on constant action and excitement. No matter how much energy she expended as co-captain of the

Sweet Valley High cheerleading squad, there was always plenty left over for shopping, gossiping, partying, and flirting.

Their attitudes toward Prince Arthur were a good example of the differences between the two sisters. Elizabeth and the prince had become special friends during his previous stay in Sweet Valley. Arthur had felt comfortable with Elizabeth because she treated him like a normal kid; she had liked him for himself, not for his title as crown prince of Santa Dora, a tiny kingdom on the Mediterranean seacoast between southern France and northern Spain. The two had corresponded ever since, and recently Elizabeth had received a flurry of letters from the young prince. In the latest, he had announced his plan to stop in Sweet Valley for a few weeks as part of the world tour he was taking prior to his seventeenth birthday and official investiture as crown prince.

"I'll never forget when Arthur was here in sixth grade," Jessica reminisced while popping the top on a can of soda. "The time I was his special date to the formal reception at the embassy . . ."

"You only got to go because you're Elizabeth's twin sister," Lila said disparagingly. "He wouldn't have invited you otherwise."

"Yeah, wasn't he mad because you gave away the secret of his identity?" Amy asked.

"That's right," said Ken Matthews, captain of the high school football team. "We all thought he was just a normal foreign-exchange student. Then we found out he was the son of King Armand and Queen Stephanie!"

"He just didn't want people to make a fuss over

3

him," Elizabeth explained. "That's why he swore me to secrecy when he told me the truth about himself."

Jessica lifted her shoulders helplessly. "Could I help it that Arthur mistook me for Elizabeth and said something to me about being a prince?"

"Can you help it that you couldn't keep a secret if your life depended on it?" Lila rejoined.

"Like *you* would have kept that secret," Jessica countered hotly. "Anyway, that's all ancient history. This time around, I won't make any mistakes. And Arthur won't, either. *This* time, he's going to fall for me, not Liz!"

"He didn't *fall* for me," Elizabeth protested, shooting a look across the table at Todd. She knew her boyfriend was more than a bit suspicious about all the letters Arthur had written to her lately, and about the fact that the prince's first stop in Sweet Valley would be the Wakefield home. "We were only in sixth grade!"

"Arthur was young and didn't know any better," Jessica agreed. "On this trip, it shouldn't take him long to figure out that he and I are meant for each other."

"Whoa! What would Sam think if he heard you talking like this?" Winston asked. "Correct me if I'm wrong, but last time I checked, you two were so close it would've required surgery to pry you apart."

Jessica gave a thought to her current boyfriend, Sam Woodruff, a senior at Bridgewater High. It was true, she and Sam were very much in love. But Sam was ... Sam. Not *Prince* Sam. "Oh, he wouldn't care," she said dismissively. "Anyway,

4

he can't blame *me* if Prince Arthur just happens to be smitten by my charms."

"If you think the prince is going to give you a second glance, Jess, you're dreaming," said Lila. "These photos prove he likes high-society girls, like yours truly."

"Your dad may be a millionaire, but Arthur's got tons of money of his own," Jessica scoffed. "He's more interested in beauty and personality."

"Exactly." Lila smiled smugly. "Face it, Jess. *I'm* going to sweep the prince off his feet."

Jessica shook her head. "Not a chance. Because *I'm* getting the first shot at him. Liz and I are meeting his plane tomorrow and then he's coming over to *our* house for lunch!"

"That doesn't mean anything," Lila retorted. "You're out of your league with Arthur. I was *born* for a royal lifestyle. You wouldn't know what to do with a palace and jewels and servants."

As Jessica struggled to come up with a pointed retort, the tabloid made its way around the lunch table along with two other photos of Arthur that Jessica had "borrowed" from Elizabeth's desk drawer.

Amy sighed rapturously over Arthur's royal portrait. "Talk about handsome," she gushed. In the photo, Arthur wore a blue uniform and a sash covered with medals. His deep brown eyes confronted the camera with a regal intensity. "If he looks this good when he comes to Sweet Valley High on Monday, I might just faint."

Amy's usually good-natured boyfriend, tennis player Barry Rork, scowled at this remark.

"If you think he looks good there, check him out

5

here." Ken's girlfriend, Terri Adams, handed Amy a candid snapshot of the prince wearing swim trunks and standing on a Mediterranean beach, his dark, curly hair windswept and his muscular body deeply tanned.

Maria Santelli gazed at the picture over Amy's shoulder. "He's perfect in every way," she concluded.

Only one girl at the table wasn't swooning over Arthur's photos. "*I* think he looks a little foolish," Dana Larson commented after a brief, scornful glance at the royal portrait. "Obviously those medals on his chest are just for decoration. I bet everything about this guy is a big pose."

Dana's comment drew supportive nods from the boys. "You girls'll be disappointed in him," Barry predicted.

"From now on, I'm wearing a crown to school," Winston joked to Maria, his girlfriend. "It's the only way to get anyone's attention around here!"

"You could wear ten crowns and you'd still be closer to a frog than a prince," Lila said dryly.

"Ouch!" Winston yelped.

"You really should try to be more pleasant, Li," Jessica warned. "If you expect an invitation to visit me at Chateau Royale someday, that is."

"Dream on. You'll be visiting *me*." Lila smiled at Arthur's royal portrait. "By the time my party rolls around, there'll be pictures of Arthur and me in all the newspapers. We'll be the couple of the hour."

Jessica made a sour face. She was sick of hearing about the extravagant bash Mr. Fowler was letting Lila throw for Arthur on his final weekend in Sweet Valley. No expense was to be spared: there would be live jazz and fancy catered food, and Lila was sure to be dressed in the latest, hottest European concoction.

Jessica *was* truly glad that Lila seemed to be bouncing back from her recent traumatic experience involving their classmate John Pfeifer. Even though she had emerged from the incident unhurt, for a while Lila's self-esteem had been shot to pieces. She felt she was at least partly to blame for John's trying to rape her. The fact that the whole school had been talking about what had happened and that not everybody believed her side of the story didn't help. But Lila had stood up for herself. She had confronted John and spoken out about the issue of date rape to the entire Sweet Valley High community. It had taken an incredible amount of courage, and the counseling Lila was getting at Project Youth was really helping her put her life back together.

But being happy that Lila seemed to be taking a healthy interest in herself and in boys again didn't mean that Jessica intended to give an inch in the duel for Prince Arthur and for social supremacy at Sweet Valley High!

She knew what she had to do: fight fire with fire. "I'm going to give a party for Arthur, too," Jessica announced.

"You are?" her sister asked in surprise.

"Yes." Jessica shot a triumphant look at Lila. "And *my* party will be a week from tomorrow. Two whole weeks before yours, Li!"

Lila narrowed her eyes. "You can throw a party every single night of the week, Jess. It's not going to get you anywhere."

"We'll see about that," Jessica said coolly.

"You know, the last time Arthur was in town, he hated everybody making a big fuss over him," Ken reminded Jessica and Lila. "Remember that dumb party the Unicorns threw, with the throne and everything?"

Ken had a point. Just thinking about the Unicorns' party, with its corny Santa Doran theme, made Jessica cringe. "This party will be the exact opposite of that one," she declared. "I learned my lesson. And unlike *some* people, I'm not going to try to impress Arthur by spending a lot of money."

"You can't afford to," Elizabeth commented.

Jessica ignored her twin. "It won't be a Santa Doran party, it'll be an all-American party," she continued. "The guests will wear red, white, and blue, and I'll have American food and good old-fashioned American rock 'n' roll music for dancing."

Jessica scanned her friends' faces. She could tell everyone liked her idea—everyone but Lila. Jessica's eyes came to rest on Dana Larson, the lead singer for Sweet Valley High's hottest rock group, and she had a sudden thought. Why play boring CDs when she could have the real thing?

"Dana, would you and the Droids like to play at my party for Arthur?" Jessica asked.

Dana shook her head, her long beaded earrings jingling. "Thanks anyway, but I'd just as soon not have anything to do with all this."

"Why not? It would be great publicity, playing at a party for an international celebrity like Prince Arthur!"

"We don't need that kind of publicity," Dana said scornfully. "If you ask me, the concept of a royal family in this day and age is completely ridiculous. We're supposed to be above all that in the United States!"

The boys laughed heartily. Jessica frowned as she tried to understand Dana's viewpoint. Maybe it was natural for someone as offbeat and unconventional as Dana to find a prince completely stuffy and old-fashioned, she decided. "All the same, will you talk it over with Guy and Max and Emily and Dan?" Jessica pleaded. "In case they feel differently."

Dana shrugged. "Sure."

The bell rang, and they all bussed their trays and headed for the door. "So, what time should I come over for lunch tomorrow?" Lila inquired, falling into step beside Jessica.

"Sorry, Li," Jessica said breezily. "It's Elizabeth's lunch party, not mine. You're not invited."

Lila stomped out of the cafeteria in a huff. Jessica followed at a slower pace, daydreaming about how, at this time the next day, she would have Prince Arthur eating out of her hand. Of course, Sam would be irked when Arthur fell madly in love with her. But he would just have to share her for a while. It was part of his burden as the boyfriend of the hottest girl at Sweet Valley High. Besides, how could Sam or anyone else expect her to say no to a prince?

"Liz, I know it's my turn to cook dinner tonight." Jessica made a big show of dropping her book bag and collapsing into a chair at the kitchen table. "But will you trade with me?"

Elizabeth shook her head. "Not this time, Jess. I still have a bunch of things to do to get ready for the lunch party tomorrow. Enid's coming over in a few minutes to help."

Jessica pouted. "But *I* have a lot to do before tomorrow, too. I still haven't decided what to wear to the airport when we go to meet Arthur!"

"What a crisis!"

"It *is* a crisis," Jessica insisted. "I want to be the girl of Arthur Castillo's dreams!"

"Well, maybe the girl of Arthur's dreams would know how to cook," Elizabeth suggested with a sly smile.

Jessica stuck her tongue out at her twin. At that moment, the phone rang. Jessica jumped up from the table and reached for the receiver. "Hello? Oh, hi, Sam."

Elizabeth leaned back against the counter. As she flipped through a cookbook she overheard Jessica's conversation.

"Yeah, the prince is coming over for lunch tomorrow," Jessica said. "Some of Liz's friends will be here, too. I'd invite you, but it's her party."

"Jess!" Elizabeth hissed. "I'd love it if Sam came. Go ahead and invite him!"

Jessica turned away, pretending not to hear her twin. "Tomorrow night? Um, I'm not sure if I'm free. Go ahead and make other plans if you want and I'll call you tomorrow afternoon, OK?"

"Why'd you blow off Sam like that?" Elizabeth asked as soon as Jessica hung up the phone.

"I didn't blow him off," Jessica said. "I just don't feel like having him over for lunch, that's all."

"What about tomorrow night? I didn't know you had another date."

"I don't," Jessica admitted. "I just don't want to

10

commit myself to anything. I mean, what if Prince Arthur asks me out?"

Elizabeth burst out laughing.

"What?" Jessica demanded. "Is it so impossible that Arthur could like me?"

"No, it's not impossible," Elizabeth said. "But where would that leave Sam?"

The doorbell rang before Jessica could answer. As Elizabeth turned to leave the kitchen Jessica called out after her, "One thing, Liz. Is it OK if I ask Dana over for lunch tomorrow?"

Elizabeth stopped in her tracks. "Dana?"

"Yeah. I think she's looking for things to do these days, since she and Aaron broke up."

"Hmm . . . and I hear the rest of the band is psyched to play at your party, but Dana's still not going for it."

"I thought maybe if she saw Arthur in person . . ."

Elizabeth put her hands on her hips. "What happened to 'Sorry, Sam, it's Liz's party or else I'd invite you'?"

Jessica smiled sweetly. "You'd better get the door—it's probably Enid."

Elizabeth hurried into the front hall. *Jessica is really out of control,* she thought. But it wasn't only Jessica. Everyone was going nuts about Prince Arthur, and he hadn't even arrived yet! Everyone . . . including Todd. Todd seemed to grow more jealous and out of sorts every day. He was convinced Prince Arthur had ulterior motives for writing so many letters to Elizabeth and wanting to visit her. How many times was she going to have to assure him that he had nothing to worry about, that she and Arthur were just good friends?

It all made Elizabeth particularly glad to see

11

Enid. At least there was one person she could count on to stay level-headed and reasonable.

The two girls headed upstairs to Elizabeth's room. "So, have you shampooed the red carpet yet?" Enid joked as she sat down on the bed.

"We don't have one in stock. Jessica will probably just lay her body down for Arthur to walk on," Elizabeth replied dryly.

Enid laughed. "So much for the entertainment. What's on the menu?"

"Raw vegetables and dip, croissants and seafood salad, a big bowl of fresh fruit, and cookies for dessert. Does that sound OK?"

"It sounds perfect," Enid replied.

"There'll be ten people altogether." Elizabeth ticked the names off on her fingers. "Arthur, me and Todd, you and Hugh, Jessica, Ken and Terri, Penny, and Dana."

Enid raised her eyebrows. "Dana? I didn't get the impression she was dying to meet the prince!"

"She's not, but it's part of Jessica's campaign to change Dana's mind about playing at the party next weekend," Elizabeth explained. "Jessica thinks Dana will be converted simply by being exposed to his royal presence."

Enid pretended to shiver with excitement. "Actually, it *is* pretty thrilling," she said.

Elizabeth smiled. "I can't wait," she admitted. "He's really a special person—not at all snobby, despite what you might expect." Elizabeth reached over to her night table and retrieved a stack of old letters and photos. "Here's a picture of me and Jessica with Arthur at the embassy reception. And here's one I took of him the day I taught him how to roller-skate."

The photograph of a young Arthur nearly toppling from his skates brought a smile to Enid's face. "He does look pretty nice and down-to-earth . . . for a prince."

"He is," Elizabeth confirmed.

"Too bad Todd's so bent out of shape about all this."

"I know. It's ridiculous! I thought he and I had worked it all out. He has no reason to be jealous. Arthur and I are just pen pals."

The two girls were silent for several moments as Enid skimmed one of Arthur's recent letters.

"Just pen pals, huh?" Enid said after a while. "I don't know, Liz. Maybe that's how *you* see it. But it does look sort of like Arthur has a crush on you."

"A crush on me? Don't be silly," Elizabeth scoffed.

Enid glanced at another letter. "Actually, I take that back."

"I should hope so!"

"He has a *big* crush on you."

Elizabeth stared at Enid. "We're good friends, that's all. I have a special place in Arthur's memory because I was the only person who was genuinely nice to him when he was here as an exchange student."

"I think his feelings are stronger than that," Enid persisted. "I hate to argue, but . . . Listen to this." She read aloud from one of the letters. " 'Every day I find myself thinking about you more and more, Elizabeth, and I look forward more and more to our reunion. I remember Sweet Valley as a very beautiful place—the perfect setting for a very beautiful girl. The only thing I

13

would enjoy more than visiting you in California would be for you to come to *my* country. I hope you will someday.' " Enid looked up. "If you ask me, Liz, you're the whole reason for Arthur's making Sweet Valley a stop on his world tour. He's coming here to see *you*. And probably not just so you can go roller-skating!"

Elizabeth frowned. When Enid read Arthur's letter like *that*, it did sound pretty romantic.

"Does Arthur know about Todd?" Enid asked.

"I know I've mentioned Todd in my letters," Elizabeth asserted. "And I'm almost positive I referred to him as my boyfriend." She sighed ruefully. "It didn't sink in, though, huh?"

Enid shook her head. "Arthur doesn't seem to realize how serious you and Todd are. Todd's instinct about all this may be right."

"I'll just have to clear things up with Arthur at the first possible moment," Elizabeth determined. "Things sure were a lot simpler when we were all in the sixth grade!"

Two

"I can't believe I let you talk me into this," Dana said to Jessica as they walked through the crowded airport. "I could have slept late this morning!"

Jessica paused to check her reflection in a plate-glass window. She was wearing a crisp white linen minidress, a pink blazer, high heels, and more gold necklaces and bracelets than Dana could count. Dana herself had thrown on a baggy black cotton sweater and flowered leggings, a casual outfit that had earned her a disapproving look from Jessica when she squeezed into the twins' Jeep.

Satisfied with what she saw in the window, Jessica resumed her purposeful stroll. "Prince Arthur is worth missing sleep over," she promised Dana. "You'll see."

"The crown prince bit aside, Arthur's a nice guy, Dana," Elizabeth remarked. "You'll be surprised."

Dana didn't voice her disagreement; she didn't want to be rude. But she really didn't expect any

15

surprises from Arthur Castillo, crown prince of Santa Dora. *He's bound to be as snobby as they come,* she thought.

The three girls reached the gate where Arthur's plane would arrive and found it already packed with camera-wielding newspaper and TV reporters. Dana spotted Mr. Santelli, Maria's father and mayor of Sweet Valley, in the crowd of dignitaries. There was a buzz of excited voices; the air crackled with anticipation. Dana couldn't believe it. All this fuss over one sixteen-year-old boy!

"There it is," Jessica squealed, grabbing Dana's arm. "Prince Arthur's plane!"

Through the window, they watched the jet roll up to the gate. Dana glanced at her friends. A smile of anticipation brightened Elizabeth's face; Jessica was literally hopping up and down.

Suddenly, a hush fell over the waiting crowd. A tall figure stepped through the door. Flashbulbs began popping left and right.

Dana stared at the young man who was the object of so much fanfare and publicity. The prince was wearing his royal uniform. The deep-blue jacket and gold sash accented his trim, broad-shouldered physique. Waves of jet-black hair were swept back from his high forehead; his large, dark eyes seemed to jump out of his chiseled, olive-skinned face.

"He looks even more handsome than in his pictures." Jessica sighed, putting a hand to her heart.

Dana's own heart was beating a little faster than it had been a minute before. She realized she was holding her breath, and exhaled in an audible "hmph." *More handsome, maybe, but also more like some kind of silly dressed-up doll,* she thought, determined to remain skeptical.

Mr. Santelli presented Arthur with a key to the city, and a representative of the airport handed him a colorful bouquet of tropical flowers. Jessica clutched Dana's arm again. "Isn't he wonderful? Isn't he gorgeous?" she gasped, practically in a swoon. "Better than a movie star!"

Dana shook Jessica off her arm. "Really, Jessica. Get a grip!"

"Oh, please just say you'll play at my party, Dana! Please?"

"Oh, all right," Dana relented. "The Droids will play at your party. But just as a favor to you, Jessica—not because of him."

"Sssh," Jessica hissed at her. "Here he comes!"

Flanked by two bodyguards in dark suits, Arthur made his way through the admiring throng, pausing every few steps to shake a hand or sign an autograph. Suddenly, his eyes lit up with pleasure.

The prince strode forward, a broad grin on his handsome face. Dana watched as he embraced first Elizabeth and then Jessica. "At last! It's so wonderful to see you," Arthur told them, his voice warm and deep.

Jessica was struck speechless. "Welcome back to Sweet Valley," Elizabeth said, smiling. Taking Arthur's hand, she steered him toward Dana. "I'd like you to meet our friend Dana Larson. Dana, this is Arthur Castillo."

Releasing Elizabeth's hand, the prince took Dana's. He bent slightly at the waist, his eyes on her face. "I'm happy to meet you, Dana," he said in the same warm, deep voice.

"Me, too," Dana responded weakly.

The prince proceeded on his way, the twins glued to his side. As Dana trailed after them she reminded herself of all the reasons why she shouldn't be impressed by Prince Arthur. Because even though Dana would rather die than admit it, Jessica had been right. Dana's first close encounter with Arthur Castillo had taken her breath away. The crown prince of Santa Dora just happened to be one of the most gorgeous boys she had ever laid eyes on.

"Relax," Enid urged Elizabeth. "Everything's ready and everything's perfect."

Her reunion with Arthur at the airport earlier that morning had been great, and Elizabeth looked forward to renewing their friendship. But the prince had given her a pretty big hug, and when he kissed her on each cheek, Elizabeth couldn't help noticing that the kisses lasted longer than the ones he gave Jessica. "I just hope Arthur and I won't start off on the wrong foot because of what I have to tell him," she said anxiously.

"You're the most tactful person I know," Enid reassured her. "You'll find the right words."

Elizabeth smiled ruefully. "Maybe, but it won't matter if he doesn't want to hear them!"

At that moment, the doorbell rang. Elizabeth's stomach lurched. Leaving Enid to arrange the napkins and silverware in a basket, Elizabeth hurried to the front hallway. To her relief, she saw that it was Todd, Ken, and Terri. "Come on in, guys," Elizabeth greeted them. "You're the first."

"I hope we got here in time to help you out," said Terri.

"Actually, you and Ken could go in the kitchen and help Enid carry stuff out to the pool," Elizabeth told her. "We'll be eating out there."

The somewhat sulky expression Todd had been wearing recently was more pronounced than ever. *Time to set his mind at ease once and for all*, Elizabeth determined, taking Todd's hand and leading him into the family room. They sat down side by side on the couch. Elizabeth looked up into her boyfriend's eyes. "I know what you think about Arthur's motives for writing to me and coming to Sweet Valley," she began. "And I've been kind of mad at you for being so suspicious. But last night, it finally occurred to me that you could be right. Maybe Arthur *does* have intentions toward me. So I'm going to explain the situation to him the first chance I get. I'll make sure he understands that there's already a wonderful boy in my life, someone I love with all my heart."

Todd wrapped his arms around Elizabeth. "I'm sorry I've been acting like such a jerk, Liz," he said, sounding both relieved and contrite. "It kind of scared me, though. I mean, the guy's a *prince*. How can I compete with that?"

"You don't have to compete; I'd never let anyone come between us. Not a prince, not *anyone*." Elizabeth lifted her face so Todd could see how serious she was. Then their lips met in a long kiss.

The doorbell interrupted them. They jumped apart, laughing. "I almost forgot," Elizabeth said, standing up and smoothing out her skirt. "I'm giving a party!"

Five minutes later, everyone had arrived except for the guest of honor. Todd played host on the patio while Elizabeth and Jessica waited eagerly in the front hall. When the royal limousine pulled into the driveway, Jessica shrieked, "He's here!"

The twins peeked out the window. Arthur, dressed in crisp khaki trousers and a purple polo shirt, stepped from the limo. Two bodyguards accompanied him to the front door.

Jessica swung the door open. "Hi, Arthur!"

"We're so glad you could come," Elizabeth greeted him. "It was sweet of you to make time for us on your very first day in California."

Arthur smiled, his dark brown eyes glowing. "My top priority while I'm in Sweet Valley is to visit with you two," he replied. "I hope you don't mind that I've brought Justino and Paolo." Arthur indicated his bodyguards.

"Of course not," Elizabeth said. "There's plenty of food. The more the merrier!"

"Your accent is almost gone," Jessica observed to Arthur as they walked through the house.

"The benefit of so much travel," Arthur explained. "And this is another benefit," he said as they stepped through the sliding glass door to the patio. "A chance to make so many new friends."

Elizabeth introduced the prince to the people gathered by the swimming pool. "You remember Ken Matthews, don't you? He's the quarterback and captain of the Sweet Valley High football team now. And this is his girlfriend, Terri Adams—she's one of the team's managers. This is my friend Enid Rollins and her friend Hugh Grayson. Hugh lives in Big Mesa. Penny Ayala is the editor of the school newspaper—she's the one who yells at me if I'm late with my column. And you met Dana at the airport."

Dana gave Arthur a brittle smile as he shook her

hand. "I didn't get a chance to tell you then that Dana's a rock star," Elizabeth continued. "She's the lead singer for the hottest band in town, the Droids."

"Wow!" said Arthur, for a moment sounding very American.

Elizabeth turned to Todd. "And last but not least, this is my . . . my special friend, Todd."

Arthur and Todd shook hands briskly. If Arthur was curious about what Elizabeth meant by "special friend," he didn't show it. "It's nice to meet you all," he said.

Elizabeth shot a glance at Todd. "Why doesn't everybody dig into the food?" she suggested. "I'll give Arthur a quick tour of the yard and garden."

"I'll come with you," Jessica volunteered.

"No, you won't," Elizabeth told her. "Stay here and make sure everyone starts eating."

Elizabeth turned her back on Jessica's peeved frown. She and Arthur strolled to the side of the house. "We have some beautiful flowers," she said. "But they're probably nothing compared to what grows in Santa Dora."

"There *are* some things in the U.S. more beautiful than anything Santa Dora has to offer," Arthur said, his eyes on her face, not the flowers. He took her hand. "It really is wonderful to see you after all these years, Elizabeth," he murmured. "You are even more lovely in person than in your photographs."

"Oh, I'm the same kid you knew back in sixth grade," Elizabeth said lightly, stepping away so that Arthur would have to release her hand. *Tell him. Just spit it out.* "Arthur, there's something I need to tell you about myself. Maybe I didn't make

21

it clear in my letters. Todd ... Todd is my boyfriend. We've been going out for a long time and I ... I care for him very much."

A look of disappointment shadowed Arthur's handsome face as Elizabeth spoke. But when she touched his arm, her expression appealing to him for understanding, the shadow departed and he smiled gallantly. "I expected that you'd have many admirers, Elizabeth. I'll confess, though, that I hoped there wouldn't be anyone special."

Elizabeth blushed. "Well, I'm flattered."

"I'm very happy for you," Arthur assured her. "I'll enjoy getting to know Todd. He must be a terrific person if you love him."

Arthur couldn't have been more gracious, Elizabeth thought. She should have known he would be a perfect gentleman. But as they walked back around the house to the pool, he seemed preoccupied. Elizabeth opened her mouth, about to ask what was still troubling him. Then she changed her mind. No, she decided, unless Arthur chose to confide in her, she was probably better off dropping the subject. Or Todd might end up challenging Arthur to a duel yet!

Dana picked at the seafood salad on her plate. The food Elizabeth had prepared was delicious, but Dana didn't have much of an appetite.

Everyone else seemed to be relaxed and having fun, but Dana couldn't remember when she'd felt so tongue-tied and uncomfortable at a party. *But this isn't really a party*, she thought. Nibbling at a croissant, Dana eyed Prince Arthur suspiciously. *It's more like a press conference!*

Even as she thought this, though, Dana knew it

wasn't quite fair. True, the prince wasn't getting much of a chance to eat because most of the girls at the party were pestering him with questions about life in Santa Dora and his round-the-world tour. But Arthur asked a lot of questions himself, and he didn't just flirt with the girls—he talked to the guys, too.

"So, you fellows are all—what's the word?" Arthur looked to Elizabeth for help. "Jocks?"

Elizabeth laughed. "That's the word."

"Jocks," Arthur repeated. "You play football, Ken?"

Ken nodded. "Have you ever played it?"

"Football's my favorite sport, after sailing," Arthur replied. "But in Europe, when we say football, we mean what you call soccer."

Ken laughed. "So I'd better not invite you to join us at practice after school on Monday. Although it would've been fun to tackle a prince!"

"I think I'll skip it." Arthur grinned. "Thanks anyway."

Dana saw Elizabeth elbow Todd. "How about basketball?" Todd asked the prince.

"We don't play it much in Santa Dora," said Arthur. "But I've watched many American games on satellite TV. While in the U.S. I'd like very much to . . ." He paused, searching for the idiom. "To shoot some hoops."

"You really have a marvelous command of the language," Penny praised. Terri jumped up to refill the prince's plate from the buffet set up on the picnic table. Enid handed him a fresh glass of mint-garnished iced tea.

Dana was simultaneously amused and disgusted by this behavior. *Arthur must be wondering what's wrong with me,* she thought with some satisfaction. *I'm the only one not offering to peel him a grape or fan him with a palm frond!*

Arthur turned the conversation to the subject of writing, and Elizabeth's and Penny's jobs at *The Oracle.* Watching Arthur interact with the gang, Dana had to admit that the prince *wasn't* a snobby aristocrat. He was friendly, funny, considerate, and not at all pompous.

"Dana?"

The voice snapped Dana out of her reverie. "Hmm?"

Prince Arthur's intent gaze was on her now. "I was just wondering what kind of songs your band plays," he said. "We love American rock 'n' roll in Europe."

As a singer, Dana spent a lot of time in the spotlight, and she loved it. But now she wished she were invisible. She hadn't made up her mind about Prince Arthur yet and she didn't know how to respond to him.

"We play mostly original stuff," she said with a shrug. "Standard rock. You'll hear us at Jessica's party next weekend."

"Great!" Arthur said enthusiastically.

Unable to think of anything else to say, Dana dropped her eyes to her plate. Arthur moved on to Hugh, asking him about Big Mesa. *He's a real diplomat,* Dana noted wryly. She wondered how she had come across just now. Out of courtesy to Elizabeth, Dana hoped she hadn't seemed cold or rude. But then again, she hoped she hadn't seemed too warm, either. She distinctly did *not* want Arthur to mistake her for yet another member of his female fan club.

Not that it matters how I act toward him, Dana realized as she watched Jessica, Terri, Enid, and even practical, unromantic Penny buzz around the prince like bees at a honeypot. *Arthur Castillo's going to be the toast of Sweet Valley no matter what I think!*

Three

"Arthur," Lila shouted. "Excuse me, Arthur!"

Arthur looked up from the autograph book he was signing. "Hi, Lila," he said politely.

Lila fluttered her lashes. "If you're free this afternoon," she said, "I wondered if you'd like to play tennis with me at my country club, or perhaps go sailing."

"I'm booked solid all week," Arthur told her regretfully. "But thank you for the invitation."

Before Lila could ask Arthur if he would like to go to dinner instead, she was elbowed out of the way by a couple of freshmen eager to get to the prince for autographs. Muttering, Lila spun on her heel and stomped back to the nearby lunch table where she and Jessica had put their trays.

"It's Wednesday already, Arthur's *third* day at school, and I *still* haven't managed a minute alone with him," she complained. "This is starting to get ridiculous."

"Tell me about it," said Jessica. "I figured that once he found out about Liz and Todd, he'd naturally turn to *me*, Elizabeth's gorgeous twin sister. But I might as well be a piece of furniture, for all he's noticed!"

Lila shook her head. She really didn't get it. She and Jessica were by far the most attractive and popular girls in the junior class. They were used to duking it out for the attention of the best-looking guys. Sometimes Lila came out on top, sometimes Jessica. But it was always one of them. In the race for Prince Arthur's attention, though, it was a tie for last place so far!

Lila was confident she would meet with success if she could only get near the prince. But as usual, he was surrounded by dozens of worshipful students. If Arthur wasn't signing an autograph, he was posing for a picture. "Royal fever" was raging out of control.

Her expression grumpy, Lila watched as Terri Adams presented Arthur with a plate of homemade cookies. Next, Amy and Penny practically came to blows arguing about who should get to interview Arthur first. Arthur eased the tension by agreeing to interviews with both *The Oracle* and WXAB, the local TV station where Amy's mother was a sportscaster.

"Disgusting, isn't it?" Jessica commented. "The way everyone's hanging all over him."

"You were practically sitting in his lap a minute ago," Lila reminded her.

"I was not sitting in his lap!" Jessica protested. Then she smiled. "Well, maybe I was, but only because I got shoved by that girl who wanted to give Arthur a bouquet of roses."

"How's he going to carry all the junk people keep throwing at him?"

"Maybe that's what the bodyguards are for!"

Lila laughed, even though in her opinion the situation wasn't the least bit funny. Narrowing her eyes, Lila studied the prince. *Maybe he's not worth it*, she speculated. Then she sighed. He *was* worth it. He was even more perfect than she had dreamed. Outrageously handsome and elegant, rich beyond belief, and *royal!* He was worlds apart from Sweet Valley High boys, and that was almost what appealed to Lila most about Arthur. She liked the thought of making a fresh start with a boy who knew nothing about that painful incident with John Pfeifer.

I simply have to snag him, Lila determined. *And I'll get to be a princess, and some day queen of Santa Dora. . . .*

"Princess Lila," she mused out loud.

"That sounds *so* dumb," Jessica scoffed. "Princess Jessica sounds much better. Jessica Castillo— now *that* has a ring to it."

Lila snorted. "Whoever heard of a blond Mediterranean princess?" She tossed her long, wavy, brown hair. "Admit it, I look the part and you don't."

"Looking the part is one thing. Landing it is another," Jessica pointed out.

Jessica was right. Lila drummed her fingers on the table and racked her brain. She just *had* to find a way to get Arthur all to herself for an hour or two. "Do you think he ever ditches those guys?" she asked, gesturing to the table where Justino and Paolo were stationed.

Jessica snickered. "It wouldn't be so bad, Li. Just imagine—a romantic candlelit dinner for *four*."

"How annoying." Then Lila's expression grew thoughtful. She studied Justino. *He's at least forty*, she guessed. *Much too old*. But Paolo, on the other hand . . . he was twenty at most, and with that dark, curly hair and those big biceps, he was definitely a hunk. "What better way to get to a prince than through his bodyguard?" she speculated out loud.

"I think I'm going to be sick," said Dana.

"I know." Guy Chesney, the Droids' keyboard player, eyed his lunch with distrust. "The soup du jour is pretty scary. What are those things floating around in there?"

"Clams?" guessed his girlfriend, Lynne Henry. "It looks like chowder."

"No, I think it's chicken," said Dan Scott, the band's bass guitarist.

"I'm not talking about the food. I'm talking about *that*." Lifting her chin, Dana indicated the scene at the other end of the cafeteria. "I mean, doesn't it just kill your appetite? Like he can't even carry his own tray or pull out his own chair! With all those flowers, he looks like he just won the Miss America contest."

Max Dellon, the Droids' lead guitarist, picked up his club sandwich. "I thought you decided to be neutral about this prince dude. You know, take him or leave him."

"I guess I'm no good at feeling neutral about things," Dana said. "I'm telling you, with every day that passes, I get more and more . . ."

"Riled up," Emily Mayer suggested.

"Incensed," said Lynne.

"Grossed out," offered Max.

"All of the above," Dana declared. "It's not even *him* so much—it's the way he's got everybody else acting. Fawning all over him, asking for his autograph . . . Am I the only girl in the entire school who hasn't lost it?"

Guy shrugged. "Well, people just think it's cool, Dana. He's a *prince*. He lives in a castle and his parents are a king and queen. I mean, it's like a fairy tale come to life."

"It's like something out of a movie," said Dan. "He's the ultimate celebrity."

Emily gazed in Arthur's direction and sighed. "Besides, he's gorgeous." Her boyfriend shot her a dirty look. "Well, it's true!" she added defensively.

"I still think it's absurd," Dana argued. "You're supposed to admire a person because of who he is inside. It's not like he did anything to earn that title. He just got lucky at birth. So why should he expect us to kiss his feet?" she shoved back her chair. "I'm going to sit outside for the rest of the lunch period. Want to come with me, Lynne? We could work on those lyrics."

"Sure."

"I'll come, too," said Guy.

Dana started toward the door. "Um, Dana, one thing before we go," Lynne called after her.

"What?"

"Could you . . . would you . . ." Lynne blushed. "I know you met him at Elizabeth's this past weekend. Would you introduce me to Prince Arthur?"

Dana put her hands on her hips. "You *must* be kidding."

Lynne looked appealingly at Dana. "I'd just like to meet him, that's all."

"I can't believe this is happening," Dana muttered as she allowed Lynne to drag her across the cafeteria.

The crowd around Arthur thinned somewhat as Dana, Lynne, and Guy approached. Arthur smiled warmly when he recognized Dana. "Hi, Dana!"

"Hi, Arthur," she said stiffly. "Arthur, I'd like you to meet Lynne Henry and Guy Chesney. Guy plays keyboards for the Droids and Lynne is a songwriter."

Lynne stepped forward eagerly to shake Arthur's hand. "I have something for you, Prince Arthur." She pulled a piece of paper from her book bag. "A song I wrote for you."

Dana glanced at Lynne's boyfriend. Guy looked just as surprised as she was. "A song?" Dana hissed. "She wrote a *song* for him?"

Prince Arthur took the sheet from Lynne. " 'Rule My Heart,' " he read. "That sounds beautiful."

"I think you'll like it," Lynne said shyly. "We'll play it for you at Jessica's party on Saturday night."

Arthur smiled at Dana. "Thank you. I'll look forward to that."

Could he be any more smug? Dana wondered. She didn't return the prince's smile. Turning on her boot heel, she stalked out of the cafeteria, Lynne and Guy chasing after her. "I can't believe you actually wrote a song for him," she snapped at Lynne. "As if he's not vain enough already! Worst

31

of all, it probably looks like I had something to do with it. Well, I'm telling you, Lynne, there's *no way* I'm singing that song at Jessica's party."

"I thought I'd sing it," Lynne said meekly.

Dana shook her head. "I used to respect you, Lynne."

"Me, too," muttered Guy.

"Oh, come on, don't be jealous," Lynne cajoled, taking Guy's hand. "I've written dozens of songs for *you*."

Dana threw up her hands in defeat. She wished she had never agreed to play at Jessica's dumb party. *But playing at the party's one thing. I can still have my own opinion about Prince Arthur,* she thought. And Dana wasn't sure how much longer she could keep her opinion to herself.

"English is my favorite class at Sweet Valley High," Arthur said to Elizabeth and Todd as they took chairs in Mr. Collins's classroom later that afternoon. "Mr. Collins is very cool."

Elizabeth smiled. "He is," she agreed. English was Elizabeth's favorite subject, too, and Mr. Collins, who was also the faculty advisor for *The Oracle*, was her favorite teacher and a good friend.

The classroom quickly filled with students. It was a repeat of every day that week, Elizabeth noted: the girls dove for seats near Arthur while the disgruntled boys clustered in the back of the room.

Elizabeth sat at Arthur's right with Todd on her other side. Today Lila triumphed, claiming the desk to the prince's left. Jessica grabbed the chair directly behind him after tripping up Maria, who was also vying for it. Elizabeth glanced at Arthur to see his reaction to this crazed behavior. He intercepted her look. Smiling good-naturedly, he lifted his shoulders as if to say, "What can I do?"

Dana was the last person to arrive. It seemed to Elizabeth that Dana made a point of not looking in Arthur's direction as she headed straight to the back of the room to sit with the boys.

Mr. Collins entered a moment later. Sitting on the edge of his desk, he held up a paperback book. "*Hamlet,* one of Shakespeare's greatest tragedies," he said. "Tell me what you think of it."

Jessica raised her hand. "I like the fact that Hamlet was a prince," she said, gazing worshipfully at the back of Arthur's head.

Mr. Collins smiled. "Well, OK. But so what? Why does that make the story more interesting?"

"Because stories about royal families are always the most interesting," Lila contributed.

Someone in the back of the room snickered. *Looks like this is going to be a stimulating literary discussion!* Elizabeth thought wryly.

"Hmm." Mr. Collins scanned the class. "Let's dig a little deeper here. What's going on with this particular royal family? What are the family dynamics that drive the plot?"

"The guy's uncle killed his dad so he could marry his mom and become king," Winston volunteered. "Understandably, Hamlet's bummed."

Laughter rippled around the classroom. Mr. Collins grinned. Ken raised his hand next. "I get that part," he said, "but I don't really understand the character of Ophelia. I mean, she goes berserk and then kills herself just because Hamlet dumps her. That seems a little extreme to me."

"She's also upset because her father was murdered," Elizabeth reminded Ken.

"Ophelia doesn't really have a choice," stated a voice from the back of the room. "She and her family have been totally exploited by the royalty. I mean, Hamlet just used her."

Elizabeth and the others in the front of the room turned to look at the speaker. "That's an interesting interpretation, Dana," Mr. Collins said. "You want to take it any further?"

Dana did. "It's always that way with royalty," she declared. "It was worse back then because royalty was more common, but it's the same thing today. Royal families use, abuse, and sponge off the people who actually *work* for a living."

There were a few startled gasps. It was pretty obvious Dana wasn't talking about *Hamlet* anymore. Mr. Collins folded his arms across his chest. "OK, Dana, let's be up-front," he said mildly. "If you have a question for Arthur, why not ask him directly?"

Dana stared defiantly at Arthur, who had turned in his seat to face her. "OK. Who's paying for this world tour of yours, anyway?"

Elizabeth glanced anxiously at Arthur, expecting him to bristle at the insult. But Arthur took the unexpected attack in stride. "I know how it probably looks," he said to Dana. "The people of Santa Dora do support my family. But we work hard, too. Traveling around the world promoting my country's interests may sound glamorous, but it's actually pretty demanding."

Elizabeth nodded. Arthur's reply was tactful and reasonable. But Dana didn't buy it. "Yeah, it looks rough, posing for photo sessions and riding around in a limousine all day."

There were indignant murmurs from Arthur's fans. A few of the boys sitting near Dana chuckled.

Arthur was about to defend himself further, but Mr. Collins waved for quiet. "It looks like we have a real disagreement here. Now, if this were a Shakespearean play, Dana and Arthur could resolve their differences with a duel. Instead, how about a debate? Dana, Arthur, are you up for it?"

Dana and Arthur both nodded.

"Great," said Mr. Collins. "I'll give you until Friday to compose your arguments on the topic of whether monarchy has any value in the late twentieth century. And remember, no poisoned rapiers!"

When the bell rang at the end of class, the students flooded from the room, talking excitedly about the upcoming debate. Elizabeth and Todd walked out with Winston and Maria. "Dana was pretty hard on Arthur," Maria commented.

Winston disagreed. "I thought she was right on target."

"At least one girl around here still has her head on her shoulders," Todd concurred.

"Todd!" Elizabeth protested.

He grinned. "You have to admit, Liz, all this hero worship is getting out of hand."

"A debate is the perfect solution." Winston looked pointedly at Maria. "Maybe it will give people, especially people of the female persuasion, a better perspective on this royalty thing."

Elizabeth supposed she couldn't blame Todd and Winston and the other boys for feeling the way they did. And besides, the debate would definitely be interesting. Because if anyone could knock Arthur off his pedestal, Dana Larson could!

Four

The fast-paced dance tune ended with an extended guitar riff from Max. "That sounded great, guys," Dana said. "Really tight."

The Droids had met at Max's garage after school on Thursday for a jam session. They had just run through the playlist for Jessica's party, and Dana was almost looking forward to Saturday night. *After tomorrow's debate, when I'll expose Prince Arthur for the fraud he really is*, she anticipated, *he'll look pretty foolish at Jessica's!*

She replaced the microphone on the stand. "Let's split," she suggested. "Anyone feel like pizza?"

"But we forgot a song," said Dan.

"Which one?" Dana asked.

" 'Rule My Heart,' " he kidded. "Didn't that one make the playlist?"

The joke drew a guffaw from Guy and Max. "Very funny," said Dana. "I already told Lynne that if she wants to serenade Prince Charming, she can go stand under his hotel-room window. I refuse to be an accomplice to the act."

"It's actually not a bad song." Emily tossed a drumstick in the air. "It's mellow—a ballad. It'd be great for your voice, Dana."

"Well, maybe I *will* sing it for His Royal Highness." Dana smiled slyly. "To console him after I cream him in the debate tomorrow."

"He's gotta be nervous," Dan remarked. "From what I heard, you were pretty tough on him yesterday."

Dana shrugged. "I just said what was on my mind."

"That's cool," said Max. "It takes guts to express your viewpoint when it goes against the crowd."

"It sounded like the prince had a pretty good comeback, though," Emily remarked. "Aren't *you* a little worried?"

"No way," said Dana. "I've got everything on my side: logic, justice, common sense. Arthur doesn't have a prayer!"

"You're taking this pretty seriously," Max observed. "Hey, maybe you're secretly in love with this guy. You know what they say about love and hate being two sides of the same coin."

Dana felt her cheeks flame. "I am *not* secretly in love with him," she stated hotly. "And I don't hate him, either. It's nothing personal. I simply despise everything he stands for, that's all."

Max lifted his eyebrows and grinned. "It was just a theory."

Dan and Max packed up their guitars. Max locked the garage door to secure the rest of the band's equipment. "I'll meet you at Guido's," he shouted, revving his motorcycle.

Dana and the others piled into Dan's car. On the way to the pizza parlor, Dan, Guy, and Emily discussed the breakup of one of their favorite local bands. Dana, however, was lost in her own thoughts. *Why am I so psyched for this debate?* she wondered, gazing out the car window at the palm trees lining the street. Why *did* she want so badly to humble Arthur Castillo?

Dana really couldn't say. But she did know one thing. Max was way off base with that two-sides-of-the-same-coin theory. *Way* off base.

"I have butterflies," Dana confessed to Elizabeth in the girls' bathroom before English on Friday. "Kind of like I get right before going on stage."

Elizabeth tucked her hairbrush back into her shoulder bag and smiled encouragingly at Dana. "You'll be great," she predicted.

"Thanks, Liz." Dana checked her appearance in the mirror. She fluffed up her short blond hair and adjusted the neck of her loose-fitting black T-shirt dress. She *was* nervous, but just a little—just enough to keep her on her toes.

They found the classroom already full and buzzing with excited discussion about the upcoming debate. Dana and Elizabeth slipped into the last couple of empty chairs.

Mr. Collins cleared his throat. "I probably don't need to remind you that we have a special event scheduled today. Now, this is how the debate is going to work. The debaters will take turns presenting their arguments, which will then be judged by Ms. Dalton, Mr. Marks, and me."

He nodded toward the French and current-events teachers, who were sitting at the side of the classroom. "As for all of you in the audience, no clapping and absolutely *no* wagering." Mr. Collins smiled at Dana and Arthur. "OK, I'll toss a coin to determine who'll start us off. Heads or tails, Dana?"

"Heads."

Mr. Collins took a coin from his trouser pocket and flipped it into the air. "Heads it is. Are you ready?"

Dana nodded. Mr. Collins had set up a podium, but instead of standing behind it, Dana walked to the front of the room and perched casually on the edge of his desk. The butterflies in her stomach had stopped fluttering and she was feeling relaxed and energized.

Looking out at her classmates, Dana's eyes came to rest on Arthur. He sat at a middle desk, surrounded as usual by Jessica, Lila, and his other admirers. More than ever, Dana felt proud of herself for not conforming, for not being taken in by Arthur's royal pose.

"The American Revolution ushered in the age of democracy," Dana began forcefully. "Not just for the United States, but for the whole world. People stopped believing in the divine right of kings and realized they deserved to choose their own leaders, create their own laws, control their own destinies, and work for themselves rather than for the profit of others. Freedom from the tyranny of the British monarchy eventually led to the growth and success of America as a nation."

Dana paused. Some of her classmates leaned forward in their seats. "In the modern world, more than two hundred years after the American Revolution, the idea of royalty is ridiculous and completely outdated," she continued. "Imagine if we had a royal family in the United States, if instead of electing a president every four years, there was some random family that from generation to generation had the power to tell us all what to do, and who sucked millions of dollars a year out of our national treasury while they were at it!"

Jumping off the desk, Dana paced in front of her audience. "The people of Santa Dora pay the royal family just for existing. Actually, they do even more than that. They foot the bill for the Castillos' incredibly glitzy lifestyle—yachts, palaces, cars, jewels, travel. The Castillos don't pay a cent. Why should such a small country have to bear a burden like that when the money could be put to better use?"

Momentum carried Dana along, and when she wrapped up her remarks five minutes later, she could see that Mr. Collins, Ms. Dalton, and Mr. Marks looked impressed; even some of Arthur's most faithful supporters appeared to be having second thoughts.

There was scattered applause from some of the boys. Todd gave her a thumbs-up sign. As Dana returned to her seat she flashed Arthur a triumphant, challenging smile.

Dana folded her arms across her chest and watched as Prince Arthur took up his position behind the podium. He looked stiff and formal. *I really can't wait to hear this*, she thought, ready to be vastly amused by his attempts to justify himself.

"This isn't the first time I've had to defend my family and the institution of royalty," Arthur began, his tone genial. "It seems foreign and old-fashioned to a lot of people, especially to you Americans. And that's natural. Because the first point I would like to make is that Santa Dora and the United States are very different countries. They are different culturally, economically, geographically, and historically. Santa Dora is tiny—not much bigger than many large American cities. We have a homogenous population and very limited natural resources and industry. For these reasons, it makes sense that a different social and political system from yours would work in our country."

It *did* make sense. Just in time, Dana stopped herself from nodding in agreement.

"Perhaps the way the two countries differ the most is in their attitudes toward tradition," Arthur went on. "The United States was founded by people who left other places in order to find new opportunities and begin new lives. The different groups in America have preserved some of their distinct qualities and customs, but in general it seems to me that in the United States there has always been an emphasis on newness.

"In contrast," Arthur said, "we Santa Dorans have had the same traditions for centuries. We do like to keep up with the latest trends, however." The class laughed as Arthur stuck out one foot to exhibit his American athletic shoes. "But more than anything, we value our traditions. And one of those traditions, maybe the most important one of all, is the royal family. Now, let me tell you what the Castillos do for Santa Dora.

"Dana's right about the country supporting us, but we *work* for that support. All members of my family work on projects that develop education, the arts, and other philanthropic causes. We're also responsible for bringing a lot of tourism to Santa Dora, and that pumps money into the economy."

As Arthur talked he gazed around the room, his eyes occasionally resting on Dana's attentive face. There was no antagonism in his expression; both his words and his manner were open, honest, and dignified.

Against her will, Dana found her convictions wavering. Suddenly, her own position seemed somewhat shallow. Arthur's argument wasn't just theoretical. Anyone could see that he was speaking from the heart, from the experience of his whole life. *But so am I*, Dana reminded herself. *My beliefs are just as real, just as valid.*

"All in all, we give a lot more than we take," Arthur concluded at last, his voice firm. "And the Santa Doran people share my view. They possess the power to abolish the monarchy; it's their choice to preserve it. We have debated the question of whether monarchy has a place in the late twentieth century and I assert that it depends on the unique circumstances of the country. In Santa Dora, it has always had a place and always will. Thank you."

Arthur bowed slightly at the waist, then walked back to his seat. Jessica, Lila, Maria, and Amy clapped wildly.

Trying to appear nonchalant, Dana watched as the judges put their heads close together for a consultation. The butterflies were back. After a few moments, Mr. Collins stood before the class. "It's hard to pick a winner in a situation like this. It's a matter of opinion rather than a question of right versus wrong. I think we all learned something just by listening to two sides of this issue. Dana

42

presented a persuasive argument. But because Arthur answered every one of her points and then some, the judges declare him the winner."

The class burst into applause. People jumped up to shake Arthur's hand and pound him on the back.

"You did a great job, Dana," Todd said.

Dana barely heard him. She really wasn't surprised by the judges' verdict. She had wanted very much to win and still had faith in her own opinion, but she was ready to admit that Arthur's case had been superior. *So why do I feel like I'm about to burst into tears?* she wondered.

As Dana rose to her feet Arthur turned to face her. Their eyes met, and in that instant Dana realized something very disturbing. It wasn't the debate that had turned her topsy-turvy . . . it was her opponent.

A warm smile crossed the prince's face. Taking a step toward Dana, he held out his hand in a friendly fashion. "Dana, I'd like to— "

The bell rang before he could finish his sentence. Dana stared at Arthur's hand. She couldn't shake it. She couldn't touch him. If she did . . . Grabbing her books, Dana bolted from the classroom, hoping to hide her confusion from her classmates, from Arthur—and from herself.

Five

Jessica squeezed Arthur's arm, thrilled to have an excuse to touch him. "That was the best debate I've ever heard," she gushed. "I mean, *your* part of it was the best."

"You were masterful," Lila purred, pushing Amy out of the way in order to take control of Arthur's other arm. "You really tore Dana to shreds."

"I wouldn't put it that way," Arthur said.

Wielding her elbows dexterously, Jessica managed to stay glued to the prince's side as he headed for the door through which Dana had just escaped. "I suppose Dana did OK, considering the fact that her position was totally wrong," Jessica amended. "Imagine thinking royalty doesn't make sense in the twentieth century!" She laughed loudly in order to show how absurd she thought this was. "I myself *fully* support the idea of a royal family."

"Hmm," Arthur murmured.

Jessica sensed she was losing him. "I think we should have a royal family here in the United States. They could hold some kind of nationwide contest to find the perfect family, and then that family could live in a castle, sort of like the White House."

Jessica knew she was babbling like a complete idiot, but it didn't seem to matter. Arthur hadn't heard a word she said. He was staring down the hallway, a puzzled, disappointed expression on his gorgeous face. Peeved, Jessica turned to see what he was looking at.

Arthur's eyes were following Dana's haughty figure down the corridor. He took a step, as if he wanted to chase after her. Jessica wrinkled her nose. Why would Arthur waste a thought on Dana Larson? "You know, Dana isn't like *most* American girls," Jessica hurried to inform the prince.

For the first time, Arthur turned to look at her. "No," he said thoughtfully. "She doesn't seem to be."

Gratified to have his attention at last, Jessica treated Arthur to her prettiest smile. "I'll make it up to you for Dana's behavior at my party tomorrow night," she promised. "You'll get a taste of *real* American hospitality."

"I'm looking forward to it," Arthur said distractedly. "Now, you must excuse me. I have an appointment."

Arthur joined his waiting bodyguards. Feasting on the tiny crumb of encouragement the prince had just given her, Jessica watched them until they disappeared down the crowded hall. "Did you

45

hear that? He's looking forward to my party!" she bragged to Lila.

Lila sniffed. "He was just being polite."

Jessica refused to let Lila's sarcasm burst her bubble. True, she hadn't made much headway with Arthur that week, but then neither had Lila or any other girl. And Jessica had a distinct feeling that things were going to change the following night. *My party will be so spectacular*, she thought in anticipation. *And so will I.*

The timing of the debate really couldn't have been better, Jessica decided as she strolled to her next class. Her charms would just seem that much more delightful when compared to Dana's utter lack of taste and tact. Hopefully, hordes of reporters would crash the party and snap dozens of photos of her dancing under the stars in Prince Arthur's arms. . . .

The hard part would be keeping Sam from sticking his face in all the pictures. She would just have to hold him off until the end of the evening. Then she could smother him with kisses to make up for neglecting him while Prince Arthur was around. And that part would be fun, too!

"Chocolate milkshakes." Arthur grinned at Elizabeth. "These I remember very well from my visit five years ago."

It was Friday night and Arthur had just slid into the booth at the Dairi Burger. Elizabeth was glad that the prince had accepted her spontaneous invitation to join her and Todd for a bite to eat, though it did feel a little funny having Justino and Paolo stationed at the very next table.

"I was just about to order room service when

you telephoned," Arthur told Elizabeth. "I have a pile of papers relating to my family's American business affairs to read through." Pushing his milkshake aside, Arthur leaned forward, his eyes intent on Elizabeth's face. "But there's something I want very much to talk to you about."

"Oh, really?" Elizabeth bit into a french fry and raised her eyebrows.

"Perhaps you two can give me some advice. You see . . ." Arthur dropped his gaze, looking suddenly shy and embarrassed. "There is a girl in Sweet Valley whom I find myself very interested in."

"Arthur, that's wonderful!" Elizabeth said. "Who is it?"

"Dana," Arthur replied. "Dana Larson."

"Dana?" Elizabeth and Todd burst out in unison.

Arthur nodded. "It seems odd to you, doesn't it? She argued against me in the debate today, but that's part of the reason I find her so fascinating. I'm impressed by everything about her—her intelligence, her independent spirit, her beautiful voice, her beautiful eyes . . ."

Arthur's expression grew dreamy. Elizabeth looked at Todd. "He's flipped," Todd whispered.

"I wanted to talk to her after the debate," Arthur went on. "To call it a tie, and to see if we could try being friends even though we have different opinions. But she ran away before I could say anything to her. So what do I do now?"

Elizabeth didn't know what to say. She was glad Arthur wasn't pining over her, but it certainly was ironic. Of all the girls in Sweet Valley who would give anything to catch his eye, he had fallen for the one who was least likely to return his admiration!

"There's really no—" Elizabeth was about to say "no hope." Then she caught herself. Maybe Arthur's crush on Dana wasn't so wacky. After all, didn't opposites attract? "There's really no reason why you and Dana shouldn't hit it off, with a little help," Elizabeth said to Arthur. "Maybe we could coax her into a double date. Todd, what if we—"

"Whoa, whoa!" Todd waved his hands, cutting Elizabeth off. "Liz, don't even think about it! Remember what happened last time we fixed Dana up with somebody?"

Elizabeth grimaced. "Yeah, I remember."

"Liz and I plotted to get Dana together with Aaron Dallas, a soccer jock at school," Todd explained for Arthur's benefit. "Even though they were total opposites."

"We figured that opposites attract." Elizabeth said the words she had just been thinking in relation to a match between Dana and Arthur. "And they did, at first."

"It wasn't instantaneous, though," Todd reminded Elizabeth. "And you and I almost broke up in the process."

"Is Dana still dating Aaron?" Arthur asked.

Elizabeth shook her head. "The relationship didn't last. In the end, I guess Dana and Aaron were just too different."

"Then Dana is free." Arthur's eyes lit up with hope.

"She's free, but she probably wants to stay that way," Todd said. "Don't get me wrong, Arthur. Dana's a great girl. But she's got pretty strong opinions. I don't see her changing her mind about this royalty thing. If I were you, I wouldn't waste my time."

48

Arthur looked thoughtfully at Todd. "So you don't think it's worth it. Didn't you have to fight at all in order to win Elizabeth's heart?"

Todd looked at Elizabeth for a moment. Then he nodded.

"See? Nothing precious can be gained without effort," Arthur declared. "Dana will be at the party tomorrow night and I will just have to . . ." He paused, seeming to search for the right word.

"Go for it," Elizabeth suggested.

Arthur grinned. "Go for it," he repeated.

"I can't believe Arthur was at the Dairi Burger and you didn't call and tell me!" Jessica wailed when Elizabeth arrived home half an hour later.

"You didn't miss much." Stepping into the bathroom that connected her bedroom to Jessica's, Elizabeth squeezed some toothpaste onto her toothbrush. "We just grabbed a quick bite. He had some work to do back at the hotel. Besides, you were out shopping for stuff for the party. You weren't even home!"

"True." Jessica heaved an exaggerated sigh. "And I'm *exhausted*. I bought a ton of food and decorations. Pounds and pounds of hamburger meat and hot dogs, and bushels of apples—Mom's going to help me bake pies tomorrow."

"How all-American," Elizabeth observed through a mouthful of toothpaste.

"I spent every last penny in my savings account," Jessica admitted. "Arthur had better appreciate all the trouble I'm going to on his behalf."

Elizabeth smiled. "Oh, he will."

"What did you and Arthur talk about?" Jessica asked.

Elizabeth finished brushing her teeth before answering. "Oh, just stuff," she said vaguely. "Life, love, that sort of thing."

"*Love?*" Jessica pounced eagerly on the word. "What does Arthur think about love?"

"Well ..." Elizabeth's dimple deepened. "Let's put it this way. If he had to debate *that* subject he'd definitely argue *for* it. See you in the morning, Jess."

Before Jessica could demand more details, Elizabeth shut her bedroom door in her sister's face. Undeterred, Jessica opened the door. She watched her twin cross to her night table. Standing with her back to Jessica, Elizabeth picked up the phone and dialed. "Hi, Enid," she said. "I hope I'm not calling too late, but I just *had* to tell you something."

Intrigued, Jessica closed the door again. She knew from experience that by pressing her ear to the crack, she would be able to hear the whole conversation.

"Jessica!" a voice called from the hall.

Drat, Jessica thought. "Yeah, Mom?" she yelled back.

Alice Wakefield stuck her head into her daughter's bedroom. "I've got some clean laundry for you."

"Thanks." Jessica took the neatly folded pile of clothes and tossed it onto her bed. She sprinted back into the bathroom, hoping she hadn't missed anything interesting.

"... completely infatuated with her. Todd and I were speechless," Elizabeth was saying.

Completely infatuated? Jessica's ears pricked up.

"Don't you think it's wild?" Elizabeth asked

50

Enid. "I mean, I know guys go crazy over her all the time. She's spunky and beautiful and talented."

Spunky, beautiful, talented ... *Sounds like me*, Jessica thought, catching her breath. *Arthur's infatuated with me!*

"But I just didn't see it coming," Elizabeth went on. "I was too worried about Arthur having a crush on *me*. Now that I think about it, there might have been sparks between them that very first day at the airport. One thing's for sure, he's planning to make his move at the party tomorrow night."

Jessica didn't need to hear any more. She ran back into her room and flung herself on the bed, an ear-to-ear grin on her face. Sparks the very first day at the airport—that clinched it!

There were *sparks*, Jessica recalled, sighing ecstatically over the memory of her first glimpse of Prince Arthur. When he clasped her hand and kissed her on both cheeks, an electric charge had definitely passed between them. And according to Elizabeth, Arthur was going to make his move the very next night!

Jessica hugged herself. She couldn't wait. Not only was she going to host the all-time best party in the history of Sweet Valley, but she was going to receive a declaration of love from the crown prince of Santa Dora! She was about to become the most famous and universally envied sixteen-year-old on the North American continent.

Six

"Would you like to dance, Arthur?" Jessica asked, raising her voice to be heard over the music.

The prince smiled regretfully. "I promised this song to Enid. And the next one to Maria and the one after that to Terri and—"

Jessica watched as Enid—boring old Enid, of all people!—whisked Arthur to the other end of the patio, where people were dancing. Grumpily, she retreated to the buffet table, where Amy and Barry were piling condiments on their grilled hot dogs.

"Every detail is perfect," Amy praised Jessica. "This is going to go on record as the best party of the school year so far!"

"Thanks," Jessica said without much enthusiasm. She turned to look back at the scene in her backyard. On the surface, the party was all Jessica had hoped it would be. Red, white, and blue banners were draped on the fence behind the swimming pool; clusters of little flags fluttered all around the patio. Her father and her older brother, Steven, who was home from college for the weekend, had charge of the grills, where hot dogs and hamburgers sizzled temptingly. The big cloth-draped picnic table was loaded with bowls of chips, bottles of soda, juicy homemade apple pies, and red, white, and blue paper plates and napkins. Even Jessica's new bikini had stars and stripes on it.

"Everyone's having a great time," Barry observed.

"It's a blast," Jessica agreed dully. A raucous water volleyball game was taking place in the pool; dozens of people were dancing wildly to the Droids' newest tune. By any standard definition, the party was a complete success.

So why am I having such a rotten time? Jessica wondered as Barry and Amy wandered off. She stared across the pool at Arthur and Enid. At this rate, Jessica was *never* going to get her picture in the paper.

Turning back to the buffet table, she picked up two plates of apple pie and two plastic forks and started in Arthur's direction, determined to talk him into sitting out a song or two.

"Hey, you read my mind," called a familiar male voice. "I'm in the mood for dessert."

Jessica whirled, almost dropping the plates. Sam slipped an arm around her waist and nuzzled her neck. "Although I'm not sure which is sweeter," he murmured, "you or the pie!"

As usual, Sam's touch made Jessica tingle from head to toe. She fought down the urge to nuzzle him back. "Um, actually," Jessica said, wriggling out of Sam's grasp, "this is for Arthur."

Sam's affectionate smile faded and his gray eyes darkened. "Right, I keep forgetting," he said sarcastically. "There's a prince in the neighborhood. The rest of us guys might as well be invisible."

"Sam," Jessica said reproachfully. "Arthur is my guest of honor. I'm just trying to be a good hostess."

"What about being a good girlfriend?" Sam demanded.

Jessica frowned. "Wait a minute. Since when am I not living up to your definition of a good girlfriend?" she snapped. "Just because I'm not hanging all over you, you take that as a rejection?"

"That's not it and you know it," said Sam. "I don't expect you to hang all over me, but I also don't expect to have to watch you hang all over some other guy."

"It doesn't mean anything," Jessica swore. "Arthur would be offended if I didn't cater to his every wish. He's a crown prince, and crown princes expect—"

"I don't care who he is!" Sam burst out. "Look, Jessica, I've been cutting you slack all night, but I've had as much as I can take. I don't know why you even invited me, since you obviously don't want me around."

"I *do* want you around," Jessica protested.

Sam stared deep into her eyes. "No, you don't. Well, I'm outta here. Believe it or not, I have some friends back in Bridgewater who actually enjoy my company. See you."

Before Jessica could stop him, Sam stormed off through the crowd. She watched his curly blond head until it disappeared. Then she sank into a chair, still clutching the two paper plates of pie. With a sigh, Jessica rested one of the plates and forks on the ground. She took a bite from the other piece of pie. Chewing thoughtfully, she watched people going wild to one of the Droids' fastest and most irresistible tunes. Arthur was dancing with Maria while Winston stood not far off, a serious scowl on his usually amiable face. *He looks just like Sam did a minute ago*, Jessica thought. *I wonder how many other couples are going to break up before this party's over?*

Suddenly, the apple pie tasted like sawdust in Jessica's mouth. She tossed the plate in a nearby garbage can. Now that Sam had walked off, clearly not intending to come back, at least not tonight, she really couldn't help wondering if Arthur Castillo was worth it.

"What are you doing down there?"

Jessica looked up. Lila stared down at her, her hands on the hips of her red-and-white polka-dotted minidress.

"Sulking," Jessica replied.

Lila pulled up a chair. "Tell me more."

Jessica knew Lila was more likely to gloat than offer sympathy, but she didn't care. "I spent all my money on this stupid party, and I may have lost my boyfriend, too, and all for nothing. Arthur hasn't shown the least bit of interest in me outside of being charmingly polite, like he is to everybody." Jessica shook her head. "I just don't get it. I really thought . . . something Elizabeth said . . ." She sighed deeply. Then her expression brightened somewhat. "At least he's not paying any attention to *you*, either."

"I've danced with him twice," Lila informed Jessica, getting to her feet huffily. "*And* we split a hamburger."

Lila flounced off. Jessica couldn't help giggling. Splitting a hamburger—talk about clutching at straws!

Standing up, Jessica contemplated Arthur, who was now dancing with Terri. She narrowed her eyes critically. *Maybe Dana's right about him*, she speculated.

Just then, the Droids began playing a slow, romantic song. In a quick quarterback-style move, Ken dashed across the patio and swept Terri into his arms. Arthur was left standing alone.

Slowly, the prince's gaze raked the crowd of party guests. Finally, his dark, intense eyes came to rest on Jessica's face. He smiled and began making his way toward her.

Jessica's heart started beating as fast as one of Emily Mayer's drum solos. *This is it!* Instantly, she forgot all the nasty thoughts she had just been having about Arthur. He was coming to claim her for the slow dance, to take her in his arms. He did have a crush on her after all! In typical polite, princely fashion, he had waited until Sam was out of the way before making his move.

Arthur reached Jessica's side. She looked up at him expectantly. "Jessica—just the person I was looking for," Arthur said, his voice husky. "I have a question for you."

Bending, he put his face close to her ear. Jessica didn't need to hear the question; she was ready to shout out her answer. *Yes, yes, yes!*

"Jessica," Arthur whispered, his breath warm on

her cheek. "Would you ... would you please ask Dana to dance the next song with me?"

"Will I *what?*" Jessica squeaked.

Arthur smiled sheepishly. "I'm afraid to ask her myself. I've been trying to get up the nerve all evening, but if I wait much longer, the party will be over."

"Dana," Jessica said in disbelief. "You want *me* to ask *Dana* to dance with you?" Jessica couldn't believe they were actually having this conversation.

"Will you help me, Jessica?" Arthur repeated.

Gritting her teeth, Jessica forced a smile. She was tempted to help him, all right—to help him right into the swimming pool!

With a tremendous effort, Jessica restrained herself. Maybe if she did this favor for him, this incredibly huge and humiliating favor, Arthur would see what a sweet, caring person she was. Then when Dana refused to dance with him, which of course she would, Jessica would be there to console him.

"As soon as this song is over, I'll talk to her," Jessica grumbled.

Dana handed the microphone to Lynne. "Your turn," she said. "I'm starved—I'm going to grab something to eat. Be back in three songs."

Dana was intercepted on the way to the buffet table by Jessica. "Dana, I need to talk to you."

"Sure, Jess. What's up?"

"Um, look, Dana," Jessica said. "Will you dance with Arthur?"

Dana stared at Jessica. "What?"

"Dance with Arthur," Jessica repeated impatiently. "He wants to dance with you. He asked me to ask you."

Dana's heart skipped a beat. She felt her face flood with color. "Really?"

"Really." Jessica folded her arms across her chest and tapped her foot. "Well, will you dance with him or not?"

Dana considered the invitation, struggling to maintain her cool, carefree attitude. It was hard when her blood was racing with excitement.

She couldn't deny it any longer. In spite of everything she had said at school, in spite of what she still believed, Dana found herself incredibly attracted to Arthur Castillo.

"Please, Dana. I don't want to stand here all night," Jessica complained. "Arthur's waiting. Do you want to dance with him or not?"

"I'm not sure," Dana hedged. It was a tougher question than Jessica realized. With any other guy, Dana wouldn't hesitate. She wasn't shy! If she liked a boy, she let him know it. But Arthur wasn't any other guy—that was the whole problem.

Dana's pounding heart urged her to seize the chance to be close to Arthur. But her head resisted the impulse. *He's not my type,* Dana reminded herself. *I should just steer clear of him.* Why did Arthur want to dance with her, anyway, when he could have his pick of all the other girls at the party? Probably just so he could gloat over his victory in the debate the day before.

But even as she thought this, Dana knew it wasn't true. Glancing across the patio in Arthur's direction, she saw him waiting for her reply, looking as nervous as any guy hoping for some encouragement from a girl he liked.

"Sure," Dana said to Jessica. "Tell him I'll dance with him."

Jessica stomped off and said a few words to Arthur. With a pleasant smile, the prince hurried to Dana's side. "Thank you for saying yes, Dana," he said, bowing slightly at the waist. "It's an honor to dance with the lead singer of the band, the most beautiful and talented girl at the party."

Dana laughed. "I bet you say that to all the girls."

Arthur's expression grew serious. "No, I don't."

Suddenly, Dana felt shy. Glad that the beat was fast so she could keep a safe distance from Arthur, she began swaying to the music. But the safety didn't last for long. The song ended, and when Lynne sang the first few bars of the next number, Dana recognized the lyrics. It was "Rule My Heart," the song Lynne had written for Arthur. It was a *slow* song.

Dana stopped, frozen with uncertainty. Arthur held out his arms. With a gulp, she stepped closer to him. Arthur took one of her hands in his and slipped his other arm lightly around her slender waist. Casually, Dana draped her free arm around his broad shoulders, hoping she didn't look as flustered as she felt.

For a minute, she avoided Prince Arthur's eyes, directing her own gaze at a point over his shoulder. Finally, though, she knew she had to look at him. When she did, the friendly, hopeful expression on his face made her laugh. "This is pretty humorous, isn't it? Considering our positions yesterday during the debate, I mean."

Arthur smiled. "I didn't even get close enough to shake your hand after class."

"I ... I'm sorry I ran off like that. I guess I

was still feeling competitive. I wasn't ready to kiss and make up yet."

Arthur's eyebrows shot up. "Kiss and make up?"

Now Dana *did* blush. "It's just a figure of speech," she explained quickly.

"Oh." Arthur's eyes twinkled mischievously. "Too bad. I would have liked that even better than a handshake!"

Dana shook her head. "I can't understand why you want to spend time with me, after all the things I said about you."

"It's really very simple," Arthur told her. "I admire you. You're independent and you think for yourself. Besides, you're a challenge," he teased. "I have to change your mind!"

"Well, I guess I admire you, too, for sticking up for yourself and for your country's traditions. *Not* that I agree with you. You can save your breath. A thousand debates couldn't convince me!"

"But you see, don't you, how Santa Dora is very different from the United States?" Arthur asked. "Tradition simply plays a different role in our lives there."

"I do see that," Dana conceded. "But even so, I still think any country, including Santa Dora, would be better off without a monarchy. Forget Santa Dora for a minute. What about *you*? Isn't being part of a royal family with tons of traditions inhibiting? All the rules you have to live by, the etiquette, the security measures . . ." Dana nodded toward Paolo and Justino, who stood watchfully at the edge of the crowd of dancers. "Answer me honestly." She looked searchingly into Arthur's eyes. "Wouldn't you rather be a carefree American teenager, free to do and think and say whatever you please?"

Arthur didn't respond right away. She could see that he was thinking seriously about her question. "Sometimes I would," he admitted at last. "At a moment like this, perhaps."

His arm tightened around her waist; a thrill ran up Dana's spine. "But more often than not," Arthur went on, "I'm grateful for the traditions of Santa Dora and of the royal family. They form the foundation of my life. They don't really limit me, as you imagine— they guide me."

Dana sensed Arthur's sincerity. But she was still dubious. "Even so . . ."

Arthur smiled. "A thousand debates before you'll change your mind?" he joked. "Then we have only nine hundred and ninety-nine left to go!"

"Ha, ha! Oh, I can't breathe."

Lila was laughing so hard, tears squeezed out of her eyes. Jessica glared at her friend. "Go ahead, have a good laugh at my expense."

Lila wiped her eyes. "That's exactly what I'm doing," she gasped. "He actually asked you to ask Dana to dance with him and you *did* it! Have you no pride?"

"Why bother with pride at that point? I was already so low, I couldn't get much lower."

"I'll say. That is *the* most pathetic story I've ever heard." Lila stifled a hiccup. "I just wish I'd been there to see the look on your face!"

"Don't forget you're a big loser tonight, too," Jessica reminded Lila. "I don't see you slow-dancing with Prince Arthur."

Together, they turned to stare at the couples

61

dancing to Lynne's sultry ballad. Arthur held Dana close. The two were talking animatedly; stars sparkled in both their eyes. "I just don't get it. Dana's supposed to be singing in the background while I slow-dance with Arthur!" She heaved a bitter sigh. "So much for becoming princess of Santa Dora."

"Things look grim," Lila admitted. "For *you*. I, for one, am not about to let the crown prince of Santa Dora slip through my fingers. Arthur can't really be interested in Dana, after all her blatant put-downs."

"What are you going to do?"

Lila pointed to Paolo, Arthur's cute young bodyguard. "It's time to put *him* to use," she declared. "I bet by making friends with him, we can find out Arthur's schedule and maybe even get invited to the hotel. If we can get Arthur alone, we can prove that Dana's all wrong for him . . . and I'm all right for him. Are you with me?"

Jessica shrugged. She supposed she might as well help Lila. Lila was more her friend than Dana was, after all. And Jessica really wouldn't mind getting back at Dana. Dana was cuddling up to Arthur and she hadn't even wanted to play at the party in the first place!

Lila marched over to Paolo, Jessica trailing in her wake. "I've been wanting to get you alone all evening," Lila informed him.

Paolo ran a hand through his curly black hair, smiling awkwardly. "You have?"

Lila stepped closer. "Yes. Jessica and I have decided that you're getting a bum deal on this trip. You have to follow Arthur everywhere and never get to have any fun on your own. How would you like to come over to my house tomorrow? For unch and a swim and maybe some tennis with ne and Jessica."

"Oh, I, well . . ." Paolo seemed overwhelmed by his sudden attention. "I'm not sure that I can. My luties to the prince—"

"Please, Paolo?" Jessica begged sweetly. "Our lay will be ruined if you don't join us."

"Well, then, I'll ask Justino for the afternoon off," Paolo resolved gallantly.

"Wonderful." Lila flashed a triumphant smile at essica. "C'mon, Paolo, let's dance."

Jessica watched Lila and Paolo whisk around the patio. *Great,* she thought. *Not only did I blow it with Arthur, but I blew it with Sam, too. And tomorrow I aave a date with the prince's bodyguard!* Things were aot turning out the way she had planned.

"I told Lynne three songs," Dana said. "I really should get back to the band."

Arthur's arms remained around Dana for a moment longer. At last he released her, but with obvious reluctance. "Thank you for the dance."

"I . . . I enjoyed it," Dana murmured.

They stepped apart, still staring deeply into each other's eyes. Finally, Dana tore her gaze from Arthur's and returned to her place behind the microphone.

She checked the playlist, then began belting out "Late Last Night," one of her favorite songs. As she sang Dana felt lightheaded and euphoric, as if her body were filled with air and she were floating above the ground.

I haven't felt this way since . . . since the last time I fell in love, Dana realized with a shock.

Something terrible was happening to her, some-

thing terrible—and wonderful. Dana's eyes sough
out Arthur. The prince stood apart from the dancers, his hands clasped behind his back. His gaze
fixed intently on her, made her blood run hot. He
was so incredibly handsome. . . .

Arthur Castillo stands for something I despise, she
reminded herself. But it didn't matter. She was
falling in love with him anyway.

Seven

"How was the party at Elizabeth and Jessica's last night?" Dana's older brother, Jeremy, asked her as she shuffled into the kitchen on Sunday morning.

"Fun." Yawning, Dana sat down at the table next to her first cousin and adopted sister, Sally. "I think you were the only girl in Sweet Valley who wasn't there, Sal."

"Mark and I went to see a play with his parents," Sally explained, passing a plate of home-made blueberry muffins to Dana. "I'm sorry I didn't get to see Prince Arthur. I know how you feel about him, but I can't help it—I think he's neat."

Jeremy gave Sally a disgusted look. "At least *you've* got some sense, Dana."

Dana smiled weakly. Sense? When it came to Arthur Castillo? Hardly.

"What's that?" Sally asked.

"What's what?" said Jeremy.

65

"That." Sally pointed out the kitchen window. "Someone just pulled into the driveway." She clapped a hand to her mouth. "Omigosh! It's Prince Arthur!"

Mr. and Mrs. Larson hurried in from the deck, where they had been drinking coffee and reading the newspaper. "There's a limousine in the driveway!" Dana's mother cried excitedly.

All color drained from Dana's face. She had dreamed about Arthur the night before, but she *hadn't* dreamed he would show up at her house!

The doorbell rang. Sally jumped to her feet.

"I'll get it," Dana said, sprinting to beat her cousin to the front hall. She had her hand on the doorknob when she remembered what she was wearing: an oversize tie-dyed T-shirt, capri leggings, and teddy bear slippers—a far cry from the chic black dress she had worn to sing at the party the night before. *I look like I just rolled out of bed, which I did, basically. Arthur probably won't recognize me.* Dana stifled a nervous giggle. *He'll take one look and hightail it back to his limo!*

She pulled the door open. Arthur stood on the stoop, looking crisp and handsome in a bright orange polo shirt and khaki Bermuda shorts. When he saw Dana, a smile as bright as the southern California sun creased his tanned face. "Good morning!"

"Hi." Dana smiled back. "Did we have a breakfast date I didn't know about?"

"I probably should have telephoned first," Arthur said sheepishly. "This was—what do you call it?—a spur-of-the-minute idea."

Dana laughed. "Spur of the moment."

"Right." Arthur grinned. "I know it's early, but

I wanted to reach you before you made other plans. I would like very much for you to spend the day with me. I hope you are free?"

Dana was flustered but thrilled by the invitation. "Oh, well, I . . ."

"You owe it to me," Arthur pressed, his eyes twinkling. "We have many more debates to conduct."

"We don't have to debate. We could just talk."

"I'd like that," Arthur said. "There's so much I want to tell you about Santa Dora."

"You know, if you really want to win me over to your point of view, you should start acting more like an ordinary person," Dana advised. "Leave the limo at the hotel!"

Arthur chuckled. "You're right. But you'll see, it can come in very handy. It can take us wherever we want to go. Please, say you'll join me."

"Well . . ." Dana couldn't resist Arthur's eager smile and warm, appealing eyes. "OK," she agreed. "Come on in while I run up and change."

Turning, she almost tripped over her family, who had snuck up behind her to eavesdrop. All four of them wore identical wide-eyed, open-mouthed expressions.

"Arthur, this is my family," Dana said. "My parents, Anne and Hal, my brother, Jeremy, and my cousin Sally. Mom and Dad, this is Arthur Castillo."

Arthur shook Mr. and Mrs. Larson's hands. Then he smiled amiably at Jeremy and Sally. "I remember meeting you both at school," he said. "It's nice to see you."

The Larsons had been struck speechless. "I'll be right back down," Dana promised. She dashed up the stairs to change. *Poor Mom and Dad*, she thought. She had given them more than their share of shocks and surprises over the years, but this topped them all. They might never recover!

Jessica opened her eyes reluctantly. The morning sun streaming in her bedroom window made her squint. *Why couldn't it rain just once?* she wondered crabbily.

She flopped over. Then she kicked her covers off and sat up. There was no point trying to fall back to sleep. She would only have more nightmares about being publicly humiliated by Prince Arthur and Dana Larson.

Someone knocked on Jessica's bedroom door. "Can I come in?" Elizabeth called.

"Sure."

She was carrying a tray with glasses of juice, bagels, and cream cheese. "Breakfast in bed," she said brightly. "I decided you deserve to be waited on, after how hard you worked last night."

Jessica sank back against her pillows. "Don't remind me!"

Elizabeth pulled up a chair next to her twin's bed. "Why not? Your party was a smash!"

"Not in my opinion. The whole point was to impress Arthur and it didn't work." Jessica grimaced. "Or maybe it worked, but not the way I meant it to. Arthur was impressed all right—by the lead singer of the band!"

"Maybe I should have warned you. I knew Arthur had a crush on Dana," Elizabeth confessed. "He told me the night before the party that he really wanted to get to know her better."

"It wouldn't have mattered," Jessica admitted, spreading cream cheese on a plump raisin bagel.

"I wouldn't have believed you. I mean, it makes absolutely no sense! I've been bending over backwards trying to cater to Arthur's every wish, saying what he wants to hear, trying to make him feel special. Meanwhile, Dana's been cutting him down left and right. And he likes her instead of me!"

"I was surprised at first, too," Elizabeth told Jessica. "But I think that's actually part of the reason Arthur likes Dana. She's up-front with him. He knows that if she's nice to him, it's not just because he's a prince. She doesn't flatter him."

Jessica let out a baffled sigh. "I still don't get it. Honesty isn't the first quality *I* look for in a guy. I'd love to go out with someone who kisses my feet and tells me I'm perfect!"

"Would you, really?"

Jessica stared at her twin. She had a feeling they were both thinking about the same person. *Sam.* Sam, who the night before had been very up-front about the fact that he thought Jessica was acting like a total jerk.

Suddenly, all the reasons she loved Sam flooded into Jessica's mind. His nutty sense of humor, the way he kissed, his reckless side, his gentle side, how he always tried his hardest to understand her even when she was being completely irrational . . .

In a flash of insight, Jessica realized she would have had a much better time at her own party if she had spent it talking and dancing with Sam, the boy she loved, instead of chasing futilely after Prince Arthur, a boy who interested her only because he was famous.

Tears sprang to Jessica's eyes. "Oh, Liz, Sam was so mad last night!" she wailed. "He'll never forgive me."

"I wouldn't be so sure of that. He was mad only because his feelings were hurt. He's crazy about you, Jess."

Jessica sniffled. "He is, isn't he?"

Elizabeth nodded. "So finish your bagel and drive over to his house and apologize!"

Thirty minutes later, Jessica rang the doorbell of the Woodruffs' home.

Mrs. Woodruff, dressed for church, answered it. "Oh, hi, honey," she said. "Go on in. Sam's in the family room."

Jessica tiptoed down the hall. Entering the family room, she found Sam slouched in front of the TV, wearing sweatpants and a ripped T-shirt. "Um, hi," she mumbled. "Sorry I didn't call first, but I figured you'd just hang up on me."

Sam started to get up, a look of pleased surprise shining in his eyes. Then he caught himself and sank back onto the couch. "Well, if I'd known you were coming, I would've worn my ermine robe and polished my scepter," he grunted.

Jessica bit her lip. "I—I guess I deserve that. I won't stay if you don't want me to. I just wanted to say I'm sorry for acting like such an idiot. You know how I always get kind of carried away by celebrities," she added wryly.

Sam snorted. "Yeah, I know. First Brandon Hunter, soap star, and now Prince Charming."

"You mean Prince Arthur," Jessica corrected him. "*You're* my Prince Charming, Sam. And you always will be."

For the first time, Sam looked up at her. Jessica waited hopefully.

"Come over here," Sam said gruffly.

Jessica crossed to the sofa. Sam pulled her down next to him. "Will you forgive me?" she asked.

Sam wrapped his muscular arms around her. "Sure, I'll forgive you," he murmured against her hair. "If you'll forgive *me* for not being able to give you tiaras and a palace and stuff like that."

Jessica hugged him back with all her might. "I don't need those things," she said honestly. "I'm incredibly lucky as it is. Because even if you do ride around on a motorcycle instead of in a royal limousine, you always treat me like a princess."

Sam squeezed her tight. Jessica sighed contentedly. It felt so right being in his arms. No other boy in the world could make her happier—she was more sure of that than ever. She lifted her face expectantly to Sam's. "So, can we kiss and make up, Prince Charming?"

In reply, Sam put his mouth tenderly on hers.

"Another sandwich, Paolo? More iced tea?"

Lila held a tray laden with overstuffed sandwiches in front of Paolo. Jessica refilled his glass.

"You don't need to go to so much trouble for me," Paolo said, choosing a turkey, cheese, and sprout sandwich.

"Oh, it's no trouble," Lila said breezily. Jessica rolled her eyes. Entertaining was never any trouble for Lila, who never lifted a finger in her own house. Fowler Crest's hired help did all the cooking and cleaning. "We're just so glad you could join us today." Lila lowered herself gracefully onto a chaise longue. "Jessica and I would have bored each other silly. But now we have someone truly fascinating to talk to!"

Lila's flattery was so obvious, Jessica was sure

Paolo would see right through it. But the poor guy seemed incredibly naive and innocent. *Or maybe just dumb,* Jessica thought. *All muscle and no brain!*

"It sure was a lucky break that you could get the day off," Lila said. "How come Prince Arthur didn't need you? Is he staying in today?"

"No. After his morning swim, he went out in the limousine with Justino to sightsee."

"He should have invited one of his new friends to go along with him," said Lila. "To tell him which sights are worth seeing."

"Oh, he was planning to do that," said Paolo. "I heard him say the first stop would be his new friend Dana's house."

Lila sat up so quickly that she practically fell off her chair. "Someone's working fast," she muttered indignantly to Jessica. To Paolo, however, she presented a perfectly sweet smile. "I'm sure Dana will be a great tour guide. For what it's worth. Sweet Valley must be the dullest part of Arthur's world tour."

"That's not true. Sweet Valley is very beautiful. The ocean reminds us of Santa Dora. And the people are nicer than in London and Paris." Paolo smiled shyly. "Arthur is having a good time here. He likes that he's not as big a celebrity in the U.S. At home, he can't go anywhere without being followed by girls who want to meet him."

"Really?" said Lila.

"They'll do anything. In Europe, girls posed as chambermaids, magazine reporters, even government officials in order to sneak into his hotel."

Lila's eyes lit up. Jessica couldn't help giggling. *Paolo's giving her some ideas!*

"Shameless," Lila said. "I can't imagine behaving that way, can you, Jess?"

Jessica shook her head. "Never."

"So, everywhere Prince Arthur goes, he's besieged by desperate women trying to meet him, huh?" Lila observed.

Paolo grinned. "It is not really so bad. I don't think Arthur would mind, if this trip were only for fun. But he has a serious matter on his mind—the traditional obligation of the crown prince on the eve of his seventeenth birthday. He knows what he must do. For the future of Santa Dora, he knows he cannot fail."

Lila shot a quizzical glance at Jessica. Jessica shrugged to indicate that she had no idea what Paolo was talking about. "The crown prince's traditional obligation? What's that?" Lila inquired.

Paolo's expression grew guarded. "A . . . task he must do."

Lila pressed for details, but Paolo would say no more about the prince's mysterious "task."

For the rest of the afternoon, Lila tried unsuccessfully to steer him back to the subject. As soon as Paolo left the two girls began to speculate.

"It sounds like Arthur's on some secret mission," said Lila. "This world tour isn't just for kicks."

"You mean, maybe even his visit to Sweet Valley has something to do with it?"

Lila nodded. "It must. And Sweet Valley is the last stop on Arthur's tour—he turns seventeen next month."

Jessica considered these facts. They didn't seem to add up to anything. "So what?"

"Oh, it's so frustrating!" Lila exclaimed. "It's like being given a puzzle with some of the pieces missing. But we've got to figure it out."

"Why?" asked Jessica.

"Because if I can find out what Arthur's secret task is, the thing that's so important to the future of Santa Dora, I can help him do it and prove to him that I'd be his perfect princess!"

"OK. But how are you going to find out what it is? Paolo won't give anything else away."

"We'll just have to investigate on our own," Lila replied. "We'll just have to get more assertive."

"*More* assertive?" Visions of dressing up as a chambermaid popped into Jessica's head. She was almost afraid to find out what Lila had in mind.

"I really should get back," Dana said. "I still have a ton of homework to do for tomorrow. The teachers always give you double over the weekend."

"No, you can't go home yet," Arthur begged. "Aren't you hungry after all that exercise? Let me buy you dinner."

Dana laughed. "I just ate a huge cheeseburger and about a million french fries. Besides, I don't find bowling all that tiring."

Arthur grinned. "It was worth a try. At least we can watch the sun set together."

They were standing next to the limousine in the parking lot of the Fast Lane, a popular new bowling alley in Sweet Valley. Now Dana turned to look at the vivid purple-and-orange western sky. "I can't believe it's this late," she said. "We've been together all day. A picnic at the beach, an old movie at the Plaza Theatre, bowling . . . aren't you sick of me yet?"

"Just the opposite. I wish this day would never end."

The warm glow of the setting sun deepened the blush on Dana's cheeks. "Still, it's been the longest date on record," she said, trying to keep the tone light.

Arthur smiled. "The longest, and the most fun."

As they climbed into the limousine they got a few stares from passers-by. Arthur caught Dana's eye and laughed. "You were right this morning," he acknowledged. "If I want to be anonymous and ordinary, I should leave the limo at home."

"I'd think you'd be constantly tempted," Dana commented. "To forget all about the crown-prince routine and goof off like you did today, I mean. Don't all those royal responsibilities make you feel old?"

"Is that how I seem to you? Old before my time?"

"Well . . . a little. Not that it's *bad* to be mature." Dana grinned. "It's a quality that sets you apart from most guys our age! But in some ways, you're missing out."

Arthur twisted in the seat to face her. "You think Santa Dora's traditions are depriving me of the freedom of youth."

"Yeah. Something like that!"

"But there are rules and laws and customs in America, too," Arthur pointed out. "For example, you're still too young to vote or enlist in the military or view certain movies, right? The way I see it, whether you live in a monarchy or a democracy, your life is shaped by traditions of some kind."

Dana flashed Arthur a challenging smile. "So tell me how *my* life is shaped by traditions."

"OK, I will. I have to learn how to run a country;

75

you have to attend school and do your homework. I live by the rules of royal etiquette and all my behavior is subject to intense international scrutiny; you must obey your parents. Elizabeth once told me what happens to Jessica when she comes home late from a date or breaks another family rule. She is like an airplane. Grounded!"

Dana laughed. "All right, I'll admit I have to toe the line at home until I'm eighteen and go away to college."

"So I win," Arthur said triumphantly.

"Not so fast! All these American rules serve a practical purpose. Whereas a lot of Santa Dora's royal customs are totally out of date, or just for show. Like that uniform you sometimes wear," Dana teased. "And the crown."

"My royal uniform?" Arthur pretended to be hurt. "You mean you don't like it? I thought for sure it would impress you!"

"Seriously, though," said Dana. "We don't have to debate *all* the time. There doesn't have to be a winner and a loser, does there?"

"No," Arthur agreed, reaching out to touch her hand.

Just then, the limo pulled up in front of the Larsons' house. Arthur walked Dana to the door. "Thank you," she said simply. "I was just kidding before, about this being the world's longest date. The hours flew by—I had a great time."

For a moment they stood close together, gazing into each other's eyes. A hopeful shiver ran up Dana's spine. Was Arthur going to kiss her? He stepped nearer and she held her breath. But instead of taking her in his arms, the prince clasped her hands in his, squeezing them warmly. "I'll never forget this day," he said. "I'd like to see you again tomorrow, Dana. And the day after that, and the day after that . . ."

Dana smiled. "I may not be able to give you another twelve hours in a row, but I'm sure we can work something out."

He held her hands for an instant longer, then released them gently. "Good night, Dana."

Dana watched the prince walk away. Suddenly, she was just as glad Arthur hadn't kissed her. It gave her one more thing to look forward to. Because Dana had a feeling she and Prince Arthur would be spending a lot more time together. The next day, and the day after that, and the day after that . . .

Eight

"No offense, Art," said Max on Tuesday afternoon, "but you're pretty much the last person I would've expected Dana to drag along to a jam session."

"Yeah, isn't this kind of a major turnaround?" Guy kidded Dana. "What happened to your anti-royalty crusade?"

"Watch out," Emily joked to the prince. "She may be trying to convert you through the power of rock 'n' roll."

"OK, OK," Dana said good-naturedly. "Go ahead, give me a hard time. Get it out of your systems. I know I deserve it!" Dana smiled at Arthur, who was taking the ribbing from her friends with good humor. "I told you they'd be harsh."

"Aw, we're not harsh." Max wrapped Dana up in a playful bear hug. "I think this is great! A small-world, global-village kind of thing."

Arthur grinned and took a seat on a stepladder in the corner of the Dellons' garage. It was the best practice session the band had had in a while; they sizzled with energy. *Is it because of me?* Dana wondered as her voice vibrated long and low on the last note of a song. Arthur didn't take his eyes off her—she felt his gaze electrify her. And when she was charged, the whole band was charged.

"That's it," Dana said after an hour. "Unless you have any special requests, Arthur."

"You didn't sing 'Rule My Heart,'" he observed.

"No. That's . . . that's Lynne's song. I don't know all the lyrics," Dana fibbed. She wasn't about to admit to her friends, much less to Arthur himself, that she had already learned the song by heart.

As usual, the royal limousine was waiting for Arthur on the street. Dana grinned as she and the prince sauntered down the Dellons' driveway. "I feel like I'm in middle-school again," she said. "Back when my parents had to drive me everywhere. Having Justino in the front seat reminds me of my very first date, with Randy Kimball. Randy's mom drove us to the movies. He and I sat together in the back seat. We may even have held hands for a few seconds!"

Arthur stopped and looked at Dana. "Justino is my guard and chauffeur, not my chaperone. He doesn't have to go *everywhere* with us."

"Oh?" Dana's eyes sparkled mischievously. "Why, what did you have in mind?"

Arthur spread his hands out. "I have no plans beyond my hope to spend as much time as possible with you," he said innocently. "What would you do now if I weren't here?"

"Probably just go out for a burger with the rest of the band."

"Ah, the Dairi Burger. I've gone there with Elizabeth and Todd. Let's go!"

"No, let's *not* go to the Dairi Burger." Dana wanted to avoid places where lots of Sweet Valley High students hung out. In her opinion, the less gossip about her and Prince Arthur, the better. "Arthur, we don't *have* to do only the sorts of things I'd do ordinarily. Your visit here is a special occasion—you should make the most of it. Maybe Justino should drive you down to L.A. and Hollywood to see the sights. I mean, aren't you getting tired of just hanging out in Sweet Valley? After all the jet-setting you're used to, it must seem pretty dull."

"Are you trying to get rid of me?" Arthur asked with a worried frown.

"Of course not. I just ... well, I guess I haven't been able to figure out why ..." Dana shrugged and turned her face away from Arthur, suddenly embarrassed. "Why me?" she finished quietly.

Arthur reached out, touching Dana's shoulder lightly. "You're wondering why I want to spend every minute with you? I'll tell you. I've done a lot of jet-setting, as you call it—you're right about that. I've traveled all around the world and met a lot of glamorous people. A lot of girls." He laughed, and Dana laughed with him. "Very beautiful, wealthy girls, and even some with royal bloodlines. But their personalities were never as magnificent as their wardrobes or the cars they drove or the parties they gave. A beautiful face isn't very interesting when the person behind it is shallow and vain. But you, Dana ..." Arthur took Dana's hand and lifted it to his lips. "You are so different. Like a breath of fresh air. You're not like other girls—you don't want to get to know me just because I am a prince. You see, you were right about something," he confessed. "My life *is* restrictive at times. But these last few days with you, I've felt liberated. I forget who I am and I just enjoy myself. Do you know what I mean?"

Dana nodded. "I think that's why I'm having such a good time, too," she admitted. "I'm not worrying about the fact that you're a prince."

"So you won't send me off to Hollywood to join the jet set?" said Arthur. "You'll let Arthur Castillo—not Prince Arthur—drive you to the beach for a swim?"

"Sure." Dana smiled. "I'd like that, Arthur Castillo."

"I do *not* want to waste another afternoon following Prince Arthur's limo around Sweet Valley," Jessica declared to Lila as they walked to the Sweet Valley High student parking lot after school on Wednesday. "I felt really stupid spying on Max's house yesterday."

Lila fumbled in her purse for the keys to the lime-green Triumph. "We didn't get caught, did we?"

"No, but the only reason Dana didn't see us cruising up and down the street in this incredibly conspicuous car is because they only had eyes for each other," Jessica pointed out bluntly.

Lila pursed her lips as she remembered the nauseating sight of Arthur kissing Dana's hand right here on the sidewalk for the whole world to see. *That should be me*, Lila thought resentfully. *I'm the one whose hand should be kissed by a prince! After what I went through with John Pfeifer, I'm the one who deserves someone like Arthur!* "Just get in the car, Jessica," she ordered.

With a peeved sigh, Jessica strapped herself into the sports car's passenger seat. "I'd bet a million dollars, if I *had* a million dollars, that Arthur will hang out with Dana again today."

"By now Dana's novelty just *has* to be wearing off," Lila said as she put on a pair of dark sunglasses and checked her reflection in the rearview mirror. Then she hit the gas, steered the Triumph out of the parking lot, and headed for Arthur's luxury hotel.

"I don't know," said Jessica. "Remember what Paolo told us when we called him last night? Arthur rearranged his whole appointment schedule for the week so he'll be free every afternoon to do things with Dana. That sounds pretty serious to me."

It did sound serious. But Lila wasn't discouraged. "Dana Larson couldn't even hold on to Aaron Dallas," she said disdainfully. "There's no way she's going to hold on to Arthur Castillo!"

"Maybe not, but I still don't think this is necessarily the best strategy," Jessica counseled. "Remember what Paolo said on Sunday? Arthur doesn't like girls who chase him."

"Oh, Paolo, Paolo." Lila waved a hand. "What does he know? Arthur's just never been chased by the right girl."

Five minutes later, Lila and Jessica entered the lobby of the bustling, elegant Palm Bay Hotel. "Just act like you belong here," Lila hissed to Jessica. "No one will stop us if we look like we know what we're doing."

She strolled toward the elevator with supreme

confidence. As she had predicted, no one gave the girls a second glance. "See how easy this is?" Lila said to Jessica as the elevator shot upward.

On the top floor, they walked down a plushly carpeted hallway. "What exactly are you planning to do?" Jessica asked apprehensively.

"This." Raising a hand, Lila rapped boldly on the door to the royal suite.

When no one responded to Lila's knock, Jessica exhaled with relief. "C'mon. Let's get out of here."

Lila tried the doorknob.

"Li!" Jessica exclaimed.

"Don't worry, it's locked. I know—let's check out the health club! Paolo said Arthur swims laps and works out every day." Lila sprinted back to the elevator with Jessica at her heels. A minute later, they were peering through the glass walls of the hotel health club at an Olympic-size swimming pool and tons of gleaming, high-tech exercise equipment. "There he is!" Lila exclaimed.

Sure enough, Arthur and Paolo were working out on the Nautilus machines. "I'm going to run down to the shops in the lobby and buy a Lycra exercise outfit," Lila declared.

"No, you are not!" Grabbing Lila's arm, Jessica dragged her away from the glass before Arthur and Paolo could spot them. "I refuse to let you make a total fool of yourself, Lila!"

Back in the parking lot, Lila drummed her fingers on the steering wheel. "There must be *something* we can do," she said, frustrated. "What about the chambermaid idea? I could borrow one of Eva's uniforms! If I could get into Arthur's suite, I might find some royal documents that would reveal his secret mission!"

"And you might get thrown in jail for breaking and entering," Jessica added sarcastically. "Look, Li, if Arthur finds out you're following him, he'll think you're a nut. It is *not* going to make him want to date you! So can we just go home?"

"No," Lila said stubbornly. "You promised you'd help me!"

"You don't need my help—you need psychiatric help."

For five minutes, the two girls argued about what—or what not—to do next. Then Lila glimpsed something out of the corner of her eye. The royal limousine was pulling up to the hotel entrance. "Look, there he goes!" Lila cried excitedly as Prince Arthur emerged from the hotel and stepped into the limo.

With a resigned sigh, Jessica sank back in her seat. Lila trailed the limousine to Dana's and parked half a block from the Larsons' house. "Now are you satisfied?" Jessica asked.

"Let's just see where they go," Lila proposed, restarting the engine as the limousine pulled away from the curb.

Keeping a safe distance, Lila followed Arthur's limo through the center of town and finally into the parking lot of the Sweet Valley Marina. The two girls watched as Arthur said a few words to Justino. Then the prince grabbed Dana's hand. Together, they ran down the dock.

"It looks like Arthur's taking Dana for a sail," Jessica observed.

"Drat," Lila said as Arthur and Dana hopped onto the deck of a sleek twenty-foot yacht. "I guess there's no time for me to stow aboard."

Jessica stared at Lila. "Stow aboard?" she repeated. "What were you hoping to do, push Dana overboard? Hijack the yacht? You have definitely cracked, Lila. Take me home *now.* You're insane and I don't want to spend any more time with you. You might be contagious!"

"What a day to be out on the water!" Dana exclaimed. She tipped her head back, relishing the sensation of the warm sun on her face and the fresh, cool ocean breeze in her hair.

Arthur pulled in the sail, causing the yacht to slice through the waves with even greater speed. "It's perfect," he agreed. "This makes me homesick for Santa Dora."

"You really know your way around a boat."

"I grew up on the water," Arthur explained. "I've been racing sailboats for years. In fact, I'm so good, I can sail with one hand. Which leaves one arm free," he added with a meaningful smile.

"Free for what?" Dana teased.

Gripping the tiller with one hand, Arthur held out his other arm. "Free for making sure my precious passenger doesn't fall overboard. Come here."

Dana joined Arthur. He wrapped his arm firmly around her shoulders, holding her close to his side. "How's that?" he asked, glancing down at her.

The wind whipped Arthur's black hair; the corners of his eyes were crinkled against the bright glare bouncing off the water. In Dana's opinion, he was absolutely the most handsome boy she had ever seen. And the nicest, too. "Just fine," she said happily.

They sat like that for a long while, without speaking, perfectly content. It was the closest physical contact she and Arthur had shared yet, and

Dana found it both exciting and comfortable. Arthur's arm around her felt strong and warm and totally right.

They reached the mouth of the bay, beyond which the sea darkened to a deep blue. "This is far enough," Arthur decided. He turned the boat into the breeze, then let out the sail. As the boat drifted gently he turned to Dana and put both his arms around her.

Dana's heart beat faster. With one hand, Arthur smoothed the hair back from her forehead. "We've been talking a lot about different traditions in Santa Dora and America," he said, his deep voice husky. "Well, there's one tradition that I believe is universal. When a boy is crazy about a girl, he wants very much to kiss her."

Dana smiled encouragingly at him. "And when a girl's crazy about a boy . . ."

Slowly, Arthur bent his head to Dana's. Their lips met in a kiss that was light and tentative at first, then warmer and deeper.

It was a magical moment. The passion they both had been suppressing flooded to the surface, and Dana gave herself to it completely. Finally, they drew apart. For a few seconds, they just gazed silently into each other's eyes. "Dana, I—"

"Yes? What is it?"

Arthur shook his head. "Nothing. Just . . . thank you."

The prince took the tiller again. Dana settled back into the crook of his arm. She sensed that he had wanted to say something to her, but he'd held it back. What could it be? *Maybe he's thinking along the same lines I am,* Dana mused. She knew it was crazy to get involved with Arthur. After all, he was in town for only a few weeks and then he would go back to Santa Dora, halfway around the world. It seemed there wasn't much future for them.

But what does the future matter? Dana thought recklessly. Hadn't she always been a risk taker, especially when it came to relationships? She definitely had a history of dating unlikely boys. And no doubt about it, Dana thought, looking up at Arthur's handsome, chiseled profile, the prince was the most unlikely but also the most wonderful boy she had ever met.

At that moment, Dana felt that her romance with Arthur was apart from time and place, like a boat on the ocean far from shore. It didn't matter that he was a European prince and she was an American high-school student who sang with a rock band. All that mattered was that they loved being with each other, that they never ran out of things to talk and laugh about.

Dana rested her head on Arthur's broad shoulder. She didn't know where this first kiss was going to lead, and she didn't care. As long as it led to a second one, and she was a hundred percent certain it would, that was enough for her.

Nine

"You're on your own," Jessica told Lila over the phone on Thursday. "I just got home from cheerleading practice and I'm pooped. I'm not interested in Arthur, *period*. If he were to walk up to my front door right now with a dozen red roses and a diamond ring, I'd tell him to—"

At that moment, the doorbell rang. Jessica, who was talking on the kitchen phone, heard Elizabeth run downstairs to answer it. "Arthur, hi," she heard Elizabeth say. "Come on in!"

"Li, he's here!" Jessica squeaked. "No, I am not kidding. He's here, in the gorgeous flesh. Get over here *fast*!"

Hanging up the phone, Jessica sprinted into the front hallway. "Well, hello, Jessica." Arthur's face lit up with an admiring smile. "It's nice to see you."

Jessica was glad she had had the foresight to change out of her sweatpants and into a bikini and shorts before calling Lila; she was sure she *was* nice to see. "Hi yourself," she said flirtatiously. "You're just in time to join me for a dip in the pool."

Arthur glanced down at his jeans. "I'm not really dressed for it. And actually . . ." He turned back to Elizabeth. "I just stopped by for a little conversation."

"Well, we can manage that, too," Jessica said. "Liz, why don't you fix some snacks? Arthur and I will go outside to the patio."

Jessica tugged on Arthur's arm, but he hung back. "That sounds like fun, Jessica, but I was hoping for a chance to talk to Elizabeth. Alone," he added.

Jessica dropped her hand from Arthur's arm. Once again, she might as well be the rug on the floor as far as Arthur was concerned. "Fine," she said stiffly. Turning on her heel, she flounced back to the kitchen. *Maybe I'll fix a snack for His Royal Highness,* she thought, seething. *Something that's sure to give him food poisoning!*

"I hope I didn't hurt Jessica's feelings," Arthur said worriedly.

Elizabeth shut the door to the den behind them. "She probably feels a little left out." She gave Arthur a reassuring smile. "But she'll get over it."

They sat down on the sofa. Elizabeth looked expectantly at Arthur, waiting for him to tell her what was on his mind. But the prince seemed at a loss for words. "It's nice to see you," Elizabeth said at last. "We haven't had a chance to talk much since you started seeing Dana."

"Dana . . ." Arthur spoke her name reverently.

89

He looked at Elizabeth, his gaze penetrating. "Elizabeth, I need advice, and there's no other person in Sweet Valley I know and trust as well as you."

"You can count on me," Elizabeth told him. "What's up?"

"It's a long story, and to you, it may also seem like a strange one," Arthur warned her. "You and I have been friends for years, but there are many things you don't know about me and my country. For example, when I wrote to tell you about my plan to visit Sweet Valley, I explained that it was traditional for the crown prince to travel the world prior to his official investiture. But I didn't mention another secret but very important reason for making this tour."

"A secret and important reason?" Elizabeth's eyes grew wide.

Arthur nodded. "As I travel around the world," he confided solemnly, "I am looking for a girl to become my wife."

Elizabeth's jaw dropped. "A girl to become your *what*?"

"My wife." Arthur raised his eyebrows. "Isn't that the right word? A girl to marry. A bride."

"It's the right word. I just can't believe it!"

Arthur grinned. "You can see why it's a secret! If word got around, there would be so much publicity. I knew you'd be surprised, Elizabeth. You do things differently here. In Santa Dora, it has long been customary for the designated crown prince to declare his betrothal before his seventeenth birthday. In this way, he demonstrates his maturity, his readiness to lead the country. It's a time-honored tradition, as old as the royal family itself."

"Wow," breathed Elizabeth. "I can't imagine getting married at the age of seventeen!"

"Well, I won't do that," Arthur assured her. "A century or two ago, the wedding would have taken place immediately. But in modern times, a long engagement has become acceptable. This is why the tradition hasn't been much noted outside of Santa Dora."

"It's certainly not common knowledge in the U.S.," Elizabeth confirmed.

"I'll wait until I graduate from college to marry, so the girl I choose will have five years to prepare, to learn the history and customs of the country prior to becoming its princess," Arthur went on. "But the engagement must be announced at the time of my formal investiture as crown prince on my seventeenth birthday. And as you know, that's very soon."

Elizabeth looked at Arthur. Over the years, they had always managed to find common ground despite their different nationalities. Now, for the first time, the prince and his world struck Elizabeth as truly foreign. "I've never heard anything like it," she said, unable to disguise her amazement. "You're traveling around the world hoping to stumble upon the perfect girl, the person you'll spend the rest of your life with? What if you don't find her?"

Arthur grimaced. "If I don't declare my own choice before my birthday, my parents will choose for me. They're eager to arrange a marriage with a member of the British royal family. But I'm determined to make my own choice." His lips curved in a smile. "And before I arrived in Sweet Valley, Elizabeth, I thought I might ask *you* to become my princess."

Elizabeth's face turned scarlet. "Me?"

"Yes, you." Arthur took her hand and squeezed it lightly. "I guess I had talked myself into being in love with you from afar," he confessed ruefully. "I saved every letter and picture you ever sent me—I could tell you were growing sweeter and more beautiful with each year that passed. But on the day I arrived, when you told me about Todd, I realized that a match with you would be impossible. And I also realized that I'd built up my memory of our childhood friendship into something it wasn't. And then—and then I met Dana. She's the one, Elizabeth."

"She is?" Elizabeth whispered.

"I'm in love with her, with everything about her," Arthur said fervently. "We're meant for each other—I'm convinced of it. But you know Dana's opinions as well as I do. I think she cares very much for me as a person, but she still thinks the idea of a royal family is ridiculous." A frustrated, discouraged note entered Arthur's voice. "This being the case, how can I ever ask her to become my betrothed?"

Elizabeth's head was spinning. Arthur had come to Sweet Valley looking for a princess and it could have been her!

Arthur waited patiently and hopefully for her advice. "I don't know what to say," Elizabeth confessed at last.

"Please," Arthur begged. "Tell me what to do."

Elizabeth smiled. "OK. If I were in your shoes, this is what I'd do. I'd talk to Dana the way you just talked to me. Be honest and straightforward. Tell her how you feel about her, and that your object is to get married. She's bound to be surprised, but if she really cares for you, she'll at least take you seriously."

"Thank you, Elizabeth," said Arthur, his eyes shining with gratitude. "You are a wise and true friend."

Elizabeth bit her lip. She hoped he would still feel that way *after* he talked to Dana!

"I feel terrible doing this," Jessica said to Lila as they sat on her twin's bed thumbing through Elizabeth's journal on Friday afternoon.

Lila snorted. "Spare me, please. Like you've never sneaked a peek in your sister's diary! You know you do it all the time."

"I just don't want to get caught."

"Don't worry, we won't. Elizabeth stayed after school to work on the newspaper, right? She probably won't be home for hours. We'll put the journal back exactly where we found it—she'll never know the difference."

It had been Lila's idea to look in Elizabeth's journal for information. When Jessica told her about Arthur and Elizabeth's private talk, it had occurred to Lila that the prince might have been seeking advice about the important task he needed to accomplish before his seventeenth birthday. Jessica had tried and failed to worm the details of the conversation out of Elizabeth. But what Elizabeth herself wouldn't reveal, her journal might. It could hold the key to Arthur's secret mission!

Lila and Jessica read quickly. "This entry mentions Arthur," Jessica exclaimed.

Lila scanned it. "It looks like she wrote it the day Arthur got here. 'I'm so glad Arthur wasn't offended when I told him about Todd,'" Lila read out loud. " 'I hope now we can enjoy spending time together as friends during the next few weeks.' " Lila shook her head in disbelief. "Sometimes I can't believe this girl is your sister. She is such a drip."

"She is not a drip!" Jessica protested. "She's just loyal to Todd."

"OK, she's not a drip," Lila amended. "She's a fool. And she keeps the world's most boring diary. What a snooze!"

"What is *with* you lately?" Jessica mumbled.

Lila ignored her and flipped rapidly through the journal, looking for the most recent entry. "Here it is!" she cried. " 'I'm still in shock over Arthur's revelation,' " Lila read. " 'I can't believe his parents, his whole country, expect him to make such a tremendous decision before he turns seventeen, just because it's traditional. How on earth will Dana respond?' "

Tantalizingly vague, the journal entry ended there. Jessica shut the book. " 'Arthur's revelation . . . a tremendous decision,' " Jessica quoted. "Sounds intense. But we already knew that much from talking to Paolo."

Lila frowned. "Except it looks like Arthur's about to bring Dana into it—whatever *it* is."

"That was the most elegant meal I've ever had," Dana said to Arthur as they strolled out of La Maison Blanche on Friday night.

Arthur lifted Dana's hands to his lips. "And you are the most elegant dinner companion I've ever had."

"You crown princes really know how to pay a compliment," she kidded.

"There's an art to it," Arthur admitted. "But in your case, it is also the simple truth." He gazed into Dana's eyes. "I wouldn't say it if I didn't mean it, Dana."

Dana squeezed his hand. When Arthur looked at her that way, she couldn't doubt his sincerity. "I know," she said softly.

As usual, the royal limousine was parked at the curb. Justino held the door for Dana. "I think we'd like to take a walk by the water," Arthur told Justino. "Would you drive us to the beach, please?"

A short while later, the limousine coasted into the nearly deserted parking lot at the municipal beach. "You may wait here for us," Arthur instructed Justino. Taking Dana's hand, he jumped from the limo. "Come on!"

They ran across the parking lot to the dunes. At the edge of the pavement, Arthur stopped and bent over. "What are you doing?" Dana asked.

"This." Arthur kicked off his shoes. Then he pulled off his socks and sprinted barefoot onto the sand. Laughing, Dana unbuckled her sandals. She left them lying with Arthur's shoes and dashed after him.

Arthur was standing by the ocean's edge. "What a night!" he exclaimed, waving a hand at the gleaming full moon that bathed the wide, sandy beach and the dark sea in a soft, magical light.

The scene was so beautiful, it took Dana's breath away. Hand in hand, she and Arthur wandered beside the water. *It's like a fairy tale*, Dana thought, her skin tingling as Arthur's shoulder brushed against hers. Walking along a moonlit beach with Prince Arthur of Santa Dora ... could anything be more impossibly romantic?

But that's not what's important, Dana reminded herself. *I'm in love with Arthur Castillo, not Prince Arthur. In love, in love* ... The words repeated joyously in her brain. It was the first time Dana had recognized how deeply she cared for Arthur. Suddenly, she longed to say the words out loud. And she had a feeling she would get a chance to. She had a feeling Arthur would say them first....

Arthur stopped walking. "Dana."

She turned to face him.

"Dana, there's something I need to talk to you about," he said, his voice unexpectedly intense.

Dana's stomach tightened into a painful knot. Suddenly, instead of being happy, she was afraid. She knew that tone. Something was wrong. *He's going to tell me we shouldn't see each other anymore.* Dana bit her lip. *He's going to point out how silly it is for us to get involved, since he'll be leaving Sweet Valley soon, and since we really belong to two different worlds.*

"Dana, will you marry me?"

The words didn't completely sink into Dana's consciousness. Her own thoughts were so dire that she was only half listening to Arthur.

Now Arthur held something out to her. Dana focused on it. She blinked. It was a velvet jewel box. "W—what did you say?" she squeaked.

"Will you marry me?" Arthur repeated. He opened the lid of the jewel box. Nestled on a bed of midnight-blue velvet was a bright gold ring with a large diamond solitaire.

Dana stared at the ring. The diamond winked back at her in the moonlight. Then she raised her eyes to Arthur's. *This can't be happening*, she thought, feeling suddenly dizzy. A marriage proposal was absolutely the last thing she had expected to hear!

In an instant, their romantic, improbable fling had become much more serious than Dana had ever dreamed possible. "You—you must be kidding," she stammered. "We met only a few weeks ago. You can't really want to marry me!"

Arthur slipped his arms around Dana's waist. "I can and I do," he said. He had never looked so earnest. "I'm in love with you, Dana. We've spent enough time together for me to be absolutely sure of that."

"I'm in love with you, too," Dana whispered. "But marriage . . ."

"It's a big commitment," Arthur acknowledged. "But I want to share my life with you, Dana. We wouldn't get married right away— we would have a long engagement so we could get to know each other better, and so you could get used to the idea of living in Santa Dora."

"Living in Santa Dora!" Dana gulped. Of course, if she married Santa Dora's crown prince, she would have to live in the palace. She'd be a princess.

"You could come to Europe for college," Arthur continued, "or I could study in the United States. And then, when we're twenty-one or so . . ." Arthur bent and brushed Dana's forehead with a tender kiss. "Say you'll be my bride," he whispered.

Dana was speechless. She loved the feel of Arthur's arms around her, the touch of his lips; she didn't want him ever to release her. But *marriage!*

Arthur was watching Dana's face closely. "This has been very sudden, and it's a big decision," he said. "I understand that you can't give me an answer right away. But Dana, if I can return to Santa Dora knowing that someday you'll be my wife, I'll be the happiest man on earth."

"I think . . . I think I need a few days to mull it over," Dana said weakly.

"Of course." Arthur took the diamond ring from the jewel box and slipped it onto the fourth finger of Dana's left hand. "Will you keep this, though, while you're deciding? I want you to carry it with you at all times as a reminder of my undying love."

Dana nodded helplessly. As Arthur kissed her again, on the mouth this time, she wondered if maybe she was dreaming this conversation, this whole night. Her life didn't just *feel* like a fairy tale anymore—it had turned into one.

Ten

Dana lay in bed on Saturday morning and watched the sun rise outside her bedroom window. She was exhausted—she'd barely slept a wink the whole night. Whenever she had started to doze off, the amazing thought struck her again and she would wake back up with a jolt. Prince Arthur of Santa Dora had asked her to marry him!

Dana hugged her pillow, remembering the romantic proposal on the moonlit beach and picturing the diamond ring she had tucked away for safekeeping in the back of her top desk drawer. With the ocean waves crashing behind him and the night wind ruffling his black hair, Arthur had never looked so irresistibly handsome.

And I do love him, Dana thought. She smiled to herself, recalling how much fun they had had together during the past week— the places they'd gone and the things they'd done, their spirited conversations, the passionate kisses ... She had never been so excited about a new relationship. Arthur was truly the boy of her dreams.

Then why am I so confused? With a troubled sigh, Dana rolled over onto her side and pulled the comforter up around her shoulders. *How come I'm not deliriously happy that the guy I love wants to spend the rest of his life with me?*

One answer to this question presented itself to her. Dana had found herself drawn to Arthur against all her expectations; it was *despite* the fact that he was a prince, not because of it. She had been ready to despise him and instead she'd fallen in love with him, but only because she had stopped thinking of him as the crown prince of Santa Dora and gotten to know him as Arthur Castillo. Now Arthur's proposal was forcing her to come to terms with the fact that Prince Arthur and Arthur Castillo were one and the same person. The boy Dana was crazy about came with a royal title, a palace in a foreign country, the works.

With another loud sigh, Dana threw back the covers and jumped out of bed. Pulling on a pair of sweatpants under the big T-shirt she slept in, she padded barefoot out into the hall. Sally's bedroom door was still closed and so was Jeremy's. *It's Saturday—they'll sleep till noon*, Dana guessed. But her parents' door was open. That meant her father was already on the golf course and her mother was downstairs.

Mrs. Larson was sitting on the deck with a cup of tea, enjoying the soft warmth of the early morning sun. Dana poured herself a cup and joined her. "You're up early," Mrs. Larson observed. "I thought you'd sleep late after your date with Arthur. Did you have a good time?"

"Yeah, we did." Dana curled up in a deck chair. She held the tea close to her face, blowing on it gently. "Arthur took me to La Maison Blanche for dinner."

"La Maison Blanche—what a treat!" Mrs. Larson gushed.

Dana shrugged. "It's just a restaurant."

"Just a restaurant!" Her mother shook her head. "La Maison Blanche is the most elegant and expensive restaurant in southern California. That young man must really want to impress you."

"I suppose." Dana eyed her mother through the steam from her tea. *Should I tell her?* she wondered. *Maybe she'll have some advice. That's what mothers are for, right?* "Mom, something else happened last night. Arthur gave me . . ." She laughed nervously. "He gave me a ring."

Her mother sat up. "He gave you a *ring*? What kind of ring?"

"A—a diamond ring. An engagement ring."

Mrs. Larson set her cup down so abruptly that it tipped over. "An engagement ring?" she gasped.

Dana nodded. "Isn't that wild?"

Mrs. Larson blinked at her daughter. Then she leapt up from her chair, tears of joy and excitement in her eyes. "Oh, honey, congratulations!" She flung her arms around Dana. "I'm so happy for you!"

"Whoa, Mom. Hold your horses!" Dana extricated herself with difficulty from her mother's embrace. "I haven't made up my mind yet."

"It sounds like a dream come true to *me*. He's a wonderful young man with a splendid future ahead of him. I mean, a *prince*! Your father and I are just so impressed with him. We couldn't hope for a more delightful son-in-law."

Dana stared at her mother. Mrs. Larson's eyes had a dreamy, faraway look in them. *Mom's just as starstruck as everybody else in town!* Dana realized. She was probably imagining the magazine photo spreads of the royal wedding, and how as Prince Arthur's mother-in-law she would be the eternal envy of all her Sweet Valley friends.

Suddenly, Dana realized how hard it was going to be to decide whether to say yes or no to Arthur. *And asking Mom for advice only confused me more. I just won't tell anyone else about Arthur's proposal,* Dana decided. It would be better to be alone with her thoughts and feelings; that way, no one else's opinion could get in the way.

"I'm not going to tell my friends or anyone about the engagement ring," Dana announced. "And promise you won't tell anyone either, Mom. Not Jeremy or Sally or Dad, and definitely not any of your friends!"

Mrs. Larson shook her head. "I don't understand why you'd want to keep such wonderful news a secret. But of course I won't say a word about it if you don't want me to."

With a sigh, Dana closed her eyes and tipped her head back so the sun could warm her face. What was she going to do?

What a wasted day, Dana thought as she hopped off the bus after school on Monday. She might as well have stayed home. She hadn't heard a single word any of her teachers had said; she was completely preoccupied with the thought of Arthur and his marriage proposal.

Nearing her driveway, it struck Dana that there were quite a few cars parked on the street—many more than usual. Then she noticed a crowd of people standing on the lawn outside the front door of her house. *That's funny*, Dana thought. *They look exactly like . . .*

Reporters.

As she walked up the driveway a dozen men and women armed with notepads, cameras, and microphones rushed toward her. "Ms. Larson, is it true?" one reporter called out. "Has Arthur Castillo asked you to marry him?"

"Will you accept his proposal?" another asked, sticking her microphone close to Dana's face.

Dana's first instinct was to run. But she was surrounded. *How on earth did they find out?* she wondered. They kept bombarding her with questions. "We heard he gave you a diamond engagement ring. Does that mean you've said yes?" "Will you marry Arthur and become a princess of Santa Dora?"

Dana took a deep breath. It looked like she would have to say something if she wanted to escape alive. "Yes, it's true that he asked me to marry him," she stated calmly. "But I haven't made a decision yet. Now, if you'll excuse me . . ."

Diving between two reporters, Dana sprinted into the garage. She found her mother in the kitchen, watching the scene through the curtain.

Dana put her hands on her hips. "Mom, how did all those reporters find out about this?" she demanded.

Mrs. Larson wilted before her daughter's penetrating gaze. "I— I'm not sure. I . . . oh, Dana, I just couldn't contain the news!" she confessed. "I ran into Irene Bacon at the market this morning and I told her. I just had to tell *someone*. But she

103

promised it wouldn't go any further and I didn't speak to another soul. I can't imagine how it got to the press so fast!"

"This is great," Dana groaned. "Everyone in the whole town probably knows by now. And if they don't know yet, they'll be reading it in the paper tomorrow!"

Dana stomped out of the kitchen, waving off her mother's apology. *This is the last thing I need*, she thought grimly. It looked like she was going to have the entire population of Sweet Valley breathing down her neck as she tried to make the toughest and most important decision of her life.

"I can't believe it," Lila declared for about the hundredth time on Tuesday. "I just can't believe it!"

She and Jessica were sitting alone at a corner table. On the opposite side of the cafeteria, Dana and Arthur were eating with some of Dana's friends. At least, Lila *assumed* the royal couple was over there. It was impossible to see them through the crowd of curious students trying to congratulate them.

"And it's all my fault," Jessica said glumly. "I just had to ask the stupid Droids to play at my stupid party. I practically threw Dana at Arthur."

Lila drummed her fingernails on the table. "Arthur and Dana fell for each other pretty fast," she said thoughtfully. "They could fall out of love just as quickly. If only I knew what Arthur's secret mission was, I *know* I could come up with a way to use that to my advantage." Suddenly, Lila had a brainstorm. "Remember those research projects we all did back in sixth grade, when Arthur came to the middle school as an exchange student?" she asked Jessica. "There were plenty of books and magazine articles at the library with information about Santa Dora and the royal family. Maybe the solution to the puzzle has been there the whole time! Jess, after school let's—"

"Leave me out of it," Jessica interjected. "I'm sick of making a fool of myself. *I* know when to jump off a sinking ship."

Lila shrugged. She really didn't need Jessica's help. And she was by no means convinced that the ship *was* sinking. It was time to do some serious research, Lila decided, her icy gaze fixed on Dana and the prince. Somehow, she would find a way to break up the happy couple and claim what was rightfully hers. Happiness.

Eleven

"News travels fast in Sweet Valley," Elizabeth remarked as she and Dana walked to their lockers after the final bell on Tuesday.

Dana laughed. "You're telling me! I should have known my mother would blab."

They reached Elizabeth's locker. Elizabeth thought Dana might continue on down the hall. Instead, Dana lingered while Elizabeth sorted through her books looking for the ones she needed for that night's homework.

Maybe she wants to talk, Elizabeth guessed. *Maybe it's OK to pry just a little!* "It's pretty romantic that Arthur proposed to you," she said. "Talk about a whirlwind courtship!"

"Isn't it wild?" Dana agreed. "I mean, I knew we'd started something special, but I just assumed it would end when Arthur left town. I never for a second thought about the future."

"He did, though."

"Yeah, he sure did. And *I'm* thinking about it now, too, believe me!"

"You must feel kind of . . . overwhelmed," Elizabeth ventured. *And pressured,* she added to herself. Arthur probably wanted an answer fairly soon, so he could announce the engagement in the traditional fashion. And that would be only the beginning. Then Dana would have to learn how to be a princess!

"Overwhelmed. That's exactly the word," Dana said. She leaned against the locker next to Elizabeth's. "Can you believe this is happening? And to me, of all people?"

Elizabeth smiled. "I really can't."

"Me neither. If it were any other guy, I'd say, what's the rush? Let's just date for a couple of years, see what happens. But Arthur's not just any other guy. Obviously!"

"No." Suddenly, Elizabeth wondered if Arthur had told Dana why he was in a rush to make their relationship official and permanent. Did she know about the Santa Doran tradition requiring the crown prince to announce his betrothal before his seventeenth birthday?

Elizabeth phrased her next remark carefully, so she wouldn't give away the fact that Arthur had sought her advice before asking Dana to marry him. "Arthur's situation *is* different."

"You mean because he's a prince? Or because he lives in another country? I think that's the reason he feels the whole thing is so urgent. Whatever we decide to do about our relationship, we'll be apart at least until high-school graduation. Arthur just wants us to be sure of each other."

As Dana spoke her brown eyes grew dreamy.

Elizabeth had never heard such a soft note in Dana's strong voice. "You two are really in love, aren't you?"

Dana nodded. "No one's ever treated me the way Arthur does. No one's ever made me feel so special."

"I'm really happy for you," Elizabeth said sincerely. "I hope everything works out the way you want it to."

Elizabeth shut her locker door. As she and Dana headed down the hall together, Elizabeth stole a look at her friend. She *was* happy for Arthur and Dana, but she was a little worried, too. Why hadn't Arthur told Dana the whole story about why he was in such a hurry to pop the question? Maybe it wouldn't matter, Elizabeth decided. Then again, maybe it would.

Dana said goodbye to Elizabeth at the door to the *Oracle* office, then hurried out of the school building. *Am I ever glad this day is over!* she thought, breaking into a run to avoid a crowd of freshman girls who looked as if they were about to descend on her.

Hoping to evade reporters, Arthur had arranged to meet Dana in the student parking lot rather than at the front entrance of the high school. Clearly, the plan hadn't worked, Dana saw as she approached the lot. There was the royal limousine, all right—literally surrounded by reporters, photographers, and curious students. Dana grimaced. It was tempting to turn around and run in the opposite direction. Instead, she took a deep breath and forged ahead.

The reporters hoisted their cameras. Dana managed an artificial smile as they clicked away. If her face had to be on the front page of the local newspaper, it might as well be a decent picture!

A dozen microphones were shoved close to her face. "Ms. Larson, we hear that just a week or two ago, you were very antiroyalty. In fact, you debated the prince on the subject. Has falling in love caused you to change your viewpoint?"

The performer in Dana rose to the occasion. *I might as well give them something for the morning edition,* she figured. "I haven't changed one bit," she responded. "And I don't intend to!"

"You mean you won't change your style if you become Arthur's princess?"

Before Dana could reply to this question, Arthur grabbed Dana's hand and pulled her inside.

Paolo hit the gas. The reporters scattered as the limo surged forward. Twisting in her seat, Dana looked through the rear window. A few reporters had jumped into their cars and were trailing the limousine in hopes of another photo opportunity. "How can we ditch them?" she asked.

"We'll drive up the coast until they give up and then turn back." Arthur slipped an arm around Dana's shoulders and hugged her close. "We'll get some time alone, just the two of us. I promise."

Dana lifted her face to Arthur's. They shared a brief, sweet kiss. "Some time alone—I'd like that," she murmured. "You and me and Paolo."

Arthur dropped a hand to Dana's waist, tickling her. "Paolo just saved us from that pack of ravenous reporters. You should be grateful."

"Oh, I am. I suppose you've been hounded like that all your life. How do you stand it?"

"I'm accustomed to it. You'll get used to it, too."

Arthur nuzzled Dana's neck. "Actually, I can relate to those reporters. I'm dying to know whether you'll say yes, too. But I promised to be a gentleman and give you all the time you need to make a decision."

Dana chuckled. "Don't worry. When the time comes, you'll be the first to know. You won't have to read it in the *Sweet Valley News!*"

"You've put my mind at ease. All in all, I'm feeling quite optimistic. You haven't said no yet, so yes must still be a possibility."

"It is." Dana brushed Arthur's face with her fingertips. Yes was a definite possibility—in fact, the word was on the tip of her tongue.

"Oh, Dana, we'll have a wonderful life together," Arthur exclaimed. "We'll travel—any adventure you've ever dreamed of having, we can have together. I'll work for Santa Dora and you can help me as much or as little as you like. The traditions won't restrict you, I promise. You can have your own career—pursue your music, do whatever you want. We'll have so much fun! And I'll cherish you, more than life itself, forever and always."

Dana wrapped her arms around Arthur's neck. They kissed passionately. Part of her was ready to accept his proposal right then and there. But even as Dana held Arthur close another part of her warned her to slow down. Becoming Arthur's wife someday would also mean becoming a princess of Santa Dora. Arthur had promised the traditions wouldn't restrict her. But how could they not? Royal responsibilities, as well as love, would shape her life. How had Arthur put it? Forever and always . . .

"You're being very patient," she murmured at last. "But I need a little more time."

Arthur nodded. "Of course. Here's a question you can answer right away, though. Will you be my date for Lila's party on Saturday?"

Dana smiled. "Yes, I will. And by Saturday night"—*four days away*, she thought—"I'll have made up my mind."

Arthur seemed satisfied with this promise. Taking Dana's hand, he lifted it to his lips. "It will be quite a party," he predicted. "I'll look forward to officially announcing our engagement to all our friends."

"Back again?" The librarian smiled at Lila. "You must be researching a very important assignment."

"Yes, it is a very important assignment," she confirmed with a sour smile. Lila didn't appreciate being reminded that she looked like a total nerd, showing up at the Sweet Valley Public Library on a Friday afternoon, the fourth afternoon in a row.

At least I don't work here, she thought as she headed to the periodical room. *Talk about pathetic!*

It took a major effort for Lila to hold onto her feeling of superiority, though. So far, all her research had come to nothing. She still didn't have a clue about Arthur's secret mission. Typing rapidly at the library's computer, Lila called up a list of magazine and newspaper articles about Santa Dora's royal family. She jotted them down, then settled herself in front of the microfiche machine.

Three hours later, her eyes were red and bleary from squinting at the tiny print. Lila dropped her head in her hands, utterly discouraged. Then she checked her delicate gold wristwatch. *I'll read one more article,* she decided. Then she would head home. Her father was having a few people over for dinner, including the publisher of the *Sweet Valley News.* Lila wanted to look her best for the occasion, just in case anything transpired at dinner that might warrant a write-up in the paper. In order to be described as radiant and glamorous rather than haggard and hideous, she would need at least an hour of heavy-duty beauty therapy.

Lila located the next article on her list, "A Day in the Life of Crown Prince Armand III." It was an article written when Arthur's father was a teenager. Lila scanned the text, pretty sure she wasn't going to find anything of interest. Then a sentence caught her eye. She read and reread the words. *This is it!* she realized, her heart pounding with sudden excitement. It was even juicier—more surprising, more significant—than she had suspected. And it explained everything—Paolo's cryptic remark the previous weekend, Elizabeth's journal entry, even Arthur's whirlwind courtship of Dana!

By far the biggest decision facing Prince Armand during his sixteenth year relates to marriage, the article stated. *In the time-honored but little-known tradition of Santa Dora, the crown prince must announce his engagement before his seventeenth birthday. If he does not, his parents, the king and queen, will choose a bride for him.*

Unbelievable, Lila thought. Arthur was obligated to get engaged before he turned seventeen. He had come to Sweet Valley looking for a wife! And of all people, he'd picked Dana. *But only because the pressure's totally on him,* Lila deduced. Dana just happened to be in the right place at the right time!

A new consideration struck Lila. Had Arthur

told his would-be bride about this interesting little tradition? *I bet she doesn't know!*

Lila jumped up and hurried to the lobby of the library. Sticking a coin in a pay phone, she quickly dialed the number of Arthur's hotel room. Paolo answered the phone. "Paolo, it's Lila Fowler," she said. "How are you?"

"I'm fine," he replied. "But Prince Arthur is not here right now. I can give him a message—"

"Actually, I was calling to talk to you."

"Really? To me?"

"I just wanted to make absolutely sure you're coming with Arthur to my party tomorrow night," Lila fibbed.

"Of course I will be there," Paolo said, sounding flattered.

"Great. We all have a lot to celebrate, don't we? It is just *so* delightful that Arthur has proposed to Dana. He must be very happy that he found a girl to marry so his parents won't have to arrange a marriage for him!" Lila kept her tone light and casual, to make it sound as if the Santa Doran marriage custom was common knowledge in Sweet Valley. She held her breath, waiting for Paolo to respond. Would he take the bait?

Paolo hesitated, but only for an instant. "It is very lucky that the prince and Ms. Larson have fallen in love," he agreed.

A minute later, Lila hung up the phone, suffused with a triumphant glow. After talking to Paolo, she was ready to wager the entire Fowler fortune that Dana Larson did *not* know about this marriage tradition.

But she'll find out soon enough! Lila determined. And then Arthur and Dana could wonder which of them had been the bigger fool: Dana for believing that the prince really loved her, or Arthur for imagining for a single minute that someone like Dana could really play the part of a princess.

How lucky Daddy's having dinner tonight with the publisher of the News! Lila had been hoping to find a way to make Dana look bad in Arthur's eyes, but making Arthur look bad to Dana would be just as effective. Lila beamed as she pictured the headlines in the next day's paper. It was really too perfect. Within hours, Dana would know she had been totally duped, Arthur would get dumped, and Lila would be there to pick up the pieces, claim her crown, and leave her life in Sweet Valley behind.

Twelve

Dana hopped out of bed on Saturday morning and stretched. A tingle of excitement ran through her from head to toe. She felt the way she used to on her birthday when she was little, bursting with anticipation of all the delightful surprises the day would bring. *Today is more special than a birthday, though*, Dana thought, slipping her arms into the sleeves of a loose terry-cloth robe. Today was the day that would decide her fate!

Downstairs, the kitchen was sun-drenched and quiet; no one else was around. Dana poured herself a bowl of cereal and a glass of juice and settled down at the table. But she couldn't eat; she was too busy daydreaming about Arthur. She had promised him her answer that evening. And with a week to consider his proposal, a week to fall more deeply in love with him, Dana was pretty sure what she was going to say.

She couldn't keep a silly grin from spreading

across her face as she thought about it. *I'm going to say yes! Arthur and I are going to be engaged!* It seemed crazy. They were still way too young to get married. But they would have a long engagement—the wedding wouldn't take place for years. In the meantime, Arthur would visit her in Sweet Valley, and she'd travel to Europe. They'd make plans to go to college together. Life would be one long adventure!

But best of all, Dana knew, was Arthur himself. She couldn't imagine ever meeting a boy she could love and respect more. It was hard for her to believe how wrong she had been about him! He wasn't an arrogant snob—he was warm, open-minded, and strong, serious yet fun-loving. *And he loves me for who I am*, Dana thought with a happy sigh. *He doesn't want me to change. He won't try to squeeze me into some royal mold.*

The phone rang, jolting Dana from her reverie. She got up to answer it. "Hello?" she said.

"May I speak to Dana?" a woman's voice requested.

A reporter, Dana guessed, wishing she hadn't taken the call. "This is Dana."

"Dana, this is Anita Solarz. I'm with the *Sweet Valley News*. I hope I didn't wake you up."

"Don't worry, you didn't. What can I do for you?"

"I won't take much of your time," Anita told her. "I was just hoping I could get you to promise that the *News* will be the first to learn if and when and how you accept Prince Arthur's proposal. We'd love to do an exclusive interview with the future princess of Santa Dora!"

116

"Sure, why not?" Dana agreed lightheartedly. "I'll tell you what—if you want to get the scoop, crash Lila Fowler's party tonight."

Anita laughed. "Thanks for the tip. And congratulations, Dana. It must be fun to be the heroine of such a romantic love story!"

"Yeah, it's fun."

"Of all the girls in the world, Arthur Castillo picked you," Anita continued enthusiastically. "And just in time!"

"Just in time?" Dana repeated.

"It's so lucky that he found someone before his seventeenth birthday," Anita explained. "It would have been a shame if he'd had to let his parents select a bride for him."

His seventeenth birthday? Let his parents select a bride? Dana had no idea what Anita was talking about, but she knew she had to find out more. "Yes, it would've been," she murmured vaguely.

Anita chatted on cheerfully. "Supposedly Prince Arthur's not at all fond of the girl Queen Stephanie and King Armand had in mind, Lady Tracy of the British royal family. But of course you know all about it."

Lady Tracy? The infamous British Brat? "Of course," Dana echoed weakly.

"It must be a wonderful feeling, knowing you have the power to make the crown prince of Santa Dora the happiest man on earth," gushed Anita. "Obviously, it means the world to Arthur to be able to return to Santa Dora after a successful world tour and formally announce his betrothal before his seventeenth birthday in the tradition of all the crown princes before him."

All the color drained from Dana's face. *The tradition of all the crown princes before him.* "Yes, it means the world to him," she confirmed.

"Well, Santa Dora couldn't ask for a lovelier princess," Anita remarked. "Good luck, Dana. Thanks for talking to me—I hope we'll speak again soon."

Dana hung up the phone. All at once, her hands and arms—her whole body—felt as heavy as lead. The sun was still shining through the kitchen window, but all the warmth had disappeared from the morning, and from her heart.

Tears of hurt and anger stung Dana's eyes as the realization sunk in. Arthur didn't love her—he had never loved her. He was just in a hurry to find a girl before his seventeenth birthday, which was only a few weeks away. All his words of love, his kisses and compliments, were just part of a game, a stupid royal tradition. *It was me or Tracy the Terrible,* Dana thought, flooded with bitter disillusionment.

The tears spilled over, running down her cheeks in two hot streams. *I should've listened to my instincts,* Dana berated herself. *How could I have let myself be fooled so badly?* Prince Arthur wasn't a person, with a real heart and real feelings. He was just a pile of stupid traditions! They were all that had ever really mattered to him—or ever would.

Dana stood at the kitchen counter crying quietly. Then her sadness and pain gave way to outrage. Running upstairs, she threw on her most ragged jeans and an ancient, faded T-shirt. *No princess look today!* she thought, sticking her feet into a pair of scuffed sandals. On her way out of her bedroom, Dana paused long enough to fumble in her desk drawer. Pulling out the velvet jewelry box, she stuffed it in her pocket.

As she backed the family car, an unglamorous station wagon, out of the garage, Dana felt liberated. *I've been riding around in that revolting royal limousine so much lately, I almost forgot who I really am,* she realized.

She sped to Arthur's hotel and parked in the first space she saw. Barging into the lobby, she nearly trampled a bellhop. She crossed to the elevator with long, purposeful strides. "Excuse me, miss," a woman at the front desk called after her. "Can I help you?"

Dana ignored her. Punching a button, she sent the elevator rocketing up to Arthur's floor. A moment later, she was knocking hard on the door to his suite.

Arthur himself opened the door. When he saw her, his eyes lit up. "Dana! What a surprise!" He reached out, ready to take her in his arms. Dana pushed him away. Arthur stumbled back into the room, his smile dissolving into a puzzled frown. "Dana, is something wrong?"

"You bet something's wrong!" she cried. "I could've just called you, but I wanted you to hear this in person. Are you ready for your answer, Prince Arthur of Santa Dora? Well, here it is. Get lost!" Dana shouted. Taking the diamond ring in its box from her pocket, she flung it at Arthur's feet. "I'm not going to the party with you tonight, I'm not going to marry you, and I never want to see you again!"

Arthur turned pale. "Dana, what's the matter? What's happened?"

"I wised up, that's what." Tears filled Dana's

eyes. "I should've known better," she cried. "I can't believe I let you sweet-talk me. You're just a typical rich boy. You think that because you're a prince, you own the world and can make people do whatever you want. And you got an extra kick out of manipulating me, didn't you? Knowing my opinions, after that dumb debate . . . Well, I'm not going to be a pawn in your sick, selfish royal game!"

Arthur stared at Dana, stunned. "Dana, I don't understand." She turned to leave, but he put out a hand and grasped her arm. "Please tell me what's happened to upset you. Give me a chance to—"

Dana yanked her arm away from him. "You've never said one honest word to me," she accused. "I'm not listening anymore." She stormed from the room, and although Arthur called desperately for her to stop, she didn't look back.

Half blinded by tears, Dana drove home, parked the car in the driveway, and bolted into the house. All she wanted now was to lock her bedroom door and be alone.

Her parents met her in the front hallway. "Honey, what's the matter?" her mother cried when she saw Dana's distraught expression.

Dana brushed past them. "I don't want to talk about it. I don't want to talk to anyone or see anyone. Especially not Arthur Castillo!" she concluded emphatically.

Upstairs, she slammed her bedroom door behind her and threw herself on the bed. Burying her face in the pillow, she burst into tears, her slender body racked by sobs.

Not more than a few minutes had passed when Dana heard the sound of a car's engine in the driveway. Sniffling, she sat up to peek through the curtain at her bedroom window. She caught her breath. It was the royal limousine! As Dana watched, Arthur hurried to the front door. The doorbell rang. A minute later, she heard her father's voice calling from downstairs. "Dana? Dana?"

She didn't answer him. Another minute passed, and then she saw Arthur walking back to the limousine. His broad shoulders were slumped. She thought she glimpsed a tear on his olive-skinned cheek.

Dana bit her lip. Arthur looked genuinely upset. *But that's just because his pride is injured, not his heart,* she thought, hardening herself against him. *He must be pretty bummed because now he'll have to marry the girl his parents pick out for him, that British Brat or someone else equally awful.*

Before stepping into the limousine, Arthur turned to take one last, sorrowful look at Dana's house. Dana drew back from the window so he wouldn't see her. As the limo drove slowly away a lump formed in her throat. Just an hour earlier, she had been euphoric. She had been on the verge of accepting Prince Arthur's marriage proposal. But now that wonderful feeling had given way to pain and disillusionment and incredible sadness. The fairy tale was over.

Thirteen

Elizabeth stood by her bedroom window on Saturday morning, towel-drying her hair. *What a beautiful day!* she thought, breathing in the heavenly scent of freshly cut grass. Everything sparkled in the sun; the fronds of palm trees swayed gently in the breeze. She decided she would work on her newspaper column for an hour or two. Then she'd see if Enid wanted to play some tennis or go to the beach for a swim. Finally, that night at Lila's party, they would all find out whether or not Dana was going to marry Prince Arthur!

Elizabeth gazed out at the street. Suddenly she blinked. The royal limousine was pulling into her driveway.

Quickly, Elizabeth dressed in khaki shorts and a bright blue tank top. She ran downstairs and opened the front door just as Arthur lifted his hand to press the bell.

Immediately, Elizabeth could see that something

was wrong—terribly wrong. Arthur's expression was distraught and his eyes were red, as if he had been crying. "Arthur, are you OK?" When Arthur didn't reply, she took his arm and pulled him into the house. "Come in and sit down."

Arthur collapsed on the living room couch. Elizabeth sat down next to him. "What's the matter?" she prompted.

"It's Dana." Arthur cleared his throat, obviously making an effort not to cry. "She . . . she just broke up with me."

Elizabeth gasped. "Oh, Arthur, I can't believe it!"

"I don't understand." Arthur's voice cracked. "She had promised that today, tonight, she'd give me her answer. And I really thought she would tell me yes. We have been so happy together—I know we could make each other happy for a lifetime. Even if she decided she didn't want to marry me, I assumed we would still love each other, still be friends. But this morning she came to the hotel—" Arthur broke off, dropping his face into his hands. "Oh, Elizabeth, the things she said! She told me she never wanted to see me again." Arthur raised tortured eyes to Elizabeth's. "She spoke as if she hated me."

Elizabeth was shocked. "I'm sure she doesn't hate you," she said. "Did she tell you why she was breaking up with you?"

"No. She just *yelled*. I don't know what could have happened to make her so mad at me! She called me selfish and said I thought I owned the world. And then she said she didn't want to be a pawn in my royal game." Arthur shook his head. "What could she have meant by that?"

"A pawn in your royal game?" It didn't mak a lot of sense to Elizabeth, either. "I don't know Arthur."

"I went to her house just now, hoping for chance to talk things over, for an explanation. Sh wouldn't come to the door." The tears Arthur ha been fighting back sparkled in his dark eyes. " love her so much, Elizabeth," he whispered. "N matter what's happened, I've just got to make h believe that. But how can I if she won't even se me?"

It was a good question. Elizabeth shook h head. "I wish I could help, but—"

"Maybe you can." Arthur clasped Elizabeth hands. "Would you talk to her?" he pleade "You're my best friend in Sweet Valley, Elizabet You're the only person I can turn to."

"Of course I'll talk to her," Elizabeth promise without hesitation. "I'll try to find out what wrong. Maybe we can patch things up betwee you two."

She spoke optimistically, but inside, Elizabe was apprehensive about her chances for succes She knew Dana, and Dana usually meant what sh said. And Dana had said she never wanted to se Prince Arthur again.

Dana sat on the edge of the bed, staring o over the front lawn with dry, aching eyes. *This w supposed to be the happiest day of my life*, she thoug dully. Instead, it was the most miserable. Dar didn't care if she ever left the house again. Aft all her show of independence and nonconformit she had become so infatuated with Prince Arth that she'd let him make a complete fool of he

How could she face the world—the press, her friends, everyone at Sweet Valley High?

Just then, a vehicle turned into the driveway. This time, it was Elizabeth's Jeep. Quietly, Dana eased open her bedroom door. She stood at the top of the stairs, listening while Elizabeth spoke to her mother. "Hi, Mrs. Larson," Elizabeth said brightly. "Is Dana home?"

"She's . . . not feeling well." The strained note in Mrs. Larson's voice was clearly audible. "I don't think she's up to seeing anybody right now. I'll tell her you came by, though."

As Dana pictured Elizabeth turning away and walking back to her car just as Arthur had an hour before, she realized she couldn't hide out forever. Sooner or later, she would have to deal with the situation and face her friends.

Elizabeth is the most sympathetic person I know. I might as well start with her, Dana thought. "It's OK," she called down to her mother. "Come on up, Liz."

Elizabeth climbed the stairs and followed Dana into her bedroom. Dana closed the door behind them. Elizabeth sat in the desk chair; Dana flung herself on her bed.

Before Dana could decide how to begin her story, Elizabeth spoke up. "Dana, Arthur just dropped by my house and told me about the fight you had. He's really upset. I'm worried about you guys. What happened?"

"Arthur used me, that's what happened," Dana declared, her eyes flashing. "I got a phone call from a reporter at the *Sweet Valley News* this morning, and guess what I found out? Arthur asked me to marry him only because there's some ridiculous tradition in Santa Dora—the crown prince has to get engaged by his seventeenth birthday. If Arthur didn't find somebody on his own during this world tour, his parents were going to make him marry Lady Tracy Windsor. Sweet Valley was his last stop, right? So he doesn't love me. He's just desperate!"

Dana watched as Elizabeth's eyes grew wide. She was glad to see that she had shocked her friend. Arthur had faked out Elizabeth, too. He'd faked out the entire town of Sweet Valley—*everyone* had thought he was such a great guy!

"I can't believe the newspaper found out about that!" Elizabeth exclaimed. "Arthur said the tradition was a carefully kept secret."

Now it was Dana's turn to gape. "Wait a minute. You mean you *knew* about this?"

Elizabeth shifted uncomfortably in her chair. "Well . . . yes," she admitted. "But only because Arthur came to me for advice before he proposed to you. He told me about the tradition. And I thought he was going to tell you about it, too."

"Well, he didn't," Dana said scornfully. "He didn't have the guts to be honest with me. Obviously he knew I'd laugh in his face if he told me the real reason he proposed!"

"Oh, Dana, please try to give him the benefit of the doubt," Elizabeth begged. "I know how it looks, but Arthur really does love you. He didn't propose to you just so his parents wouldn't make him marry Tracy the Terrible."

Dana's skepticism remained firm. "How do you know that?"

"Because he and I talked about it. It's true about the tradition. It does exist, and traditions matter to

Arthur—you know that by now. So yes, Arthur came to Sweet Valley with the idea, the hope, that he might meet the right girl here." Elizabeth smiled sheepishly. "He even thought it might be me, since we've been friends for a long time."

"What?" Dana said in disbelief. "He proposed to *you*, too?"

Elizabeth reddened. "No, of course not," she said quickly. "I mean, not exactly. The point is—"

Dana cut Elizabeth off. "Save your breath, Liz. I know you mean well, but let's face it. As far as Arthur was concerned, any girl would do!"

"That's simply not true," Elizabeth said earnestly. "Dana, if you could have seen him just now—"

Dana snorted. "I don't need to see him. I can imagine the performance he gave. What a manipulator!"

She stood up, indicating that it was time for Elizabeth to leave. Reluctantly, Elizabeth rose to her feet as well. "I really blew it," she said sadly. "Nothing came out the way I wanted it to. I wish I could convince you to give Arthur another chance. Won't you agree to talk to him just one more time?"

"I don't need to talk to him one more time. You can give him a message, though."

"Really? What?"

"Tell him ..." Dana felt tears coming on once more, but she fought them back fiercely. *I'm never ever going to cry over that boy again.* "Tell him goodbye."

Back home, Elizabeth dropped her purse and car keys on the kitchen table with a discouraged sigh.

She knew she should call Arthur at the hotel and tell him about her talk with Dana, but it was really the last thing she felt like doing.

"Liz, there you are!" Jessica bounced into the room. "What's going on? What happened between Arthur and Dana? Why did she break up with him?"

Elizabeth turned and looked suspiciously at Jessica. "How do you know they broke up?"

"Well, I just happened to come downstairs while you and Arthur were in the living room talking earlier," Jessica explained, putting on her most innocent expression. "And then I just happened to overhear him say something about a fight with Dana."

Frowning, Elizabeth folded her arms across her chest. "How many other private conversations have you just *happened* to overhear?" she asked sarcastically. "Don't tell me you're the one who spilled the secret to the newspaper?"

Jessica looked puzzled. "What secret?"

"You know what secret! The secret about the Santa Doran marriage custom."

"*What* marriage custom?"

Elizabeth couldn't believe Jessica was still playing dumb. "The tradition of the crown prince having to choose a betrothed before his seventeenth birthday or else his parents will choose one for him," she said impatiently. "Come on, Jess. Why don't you admit it? Someone told the newspaper and the newspaper told Dana, and now she's furious because she thinks Arthur proposed just so he wouldn't have to submit to an arranged marriage. It had to be you!"

"It did not have to be me!" Jessica protested.

"No one else could possibly have found out," Elizabeth argued. "You must have *overheard* Arthur and me talking last week, when he confided in me about the secret reason for his trip around the world. After all, it was you who gave away the secret of his identity back in sixth grade."

"Liz, that was five years ago!"

"So? You and Lila were plotting back then and you're still plotting. You can't deny that you've been trying to come up with a way to steal Arthur away from Dana," Elizabeth persisted. "Well, it looks like your scheme worked."

Jessica's eyes flashed with indignation. "I did not give away this secret! I mean, I might have if I'd known it," she added candidly. "But I didn't. I really can't believe you, Liz, blaming me all over again for what happened when we were in the sixth grade."

Elizabeth stared hard at her twin. Jessica returned her gaze defiantly. Elizabeth could see that her sister was genuinely offended; she wasn't faking it. "Oh, Jess, I'm sorry," Elizabeth said after a moment. "You're right, it was totally unfair of me to accuse you."

"Totally," Jessica confirmed, flouncing out of the room.

Elizabeth sank down in a chair. Leaning her elbows on the butcher-block table, she dropped her chin in her hands. If Jessica hadn't leaked the secret, then who had? Did it even matter at this point, now that Dana had found out? Probably not, Elizabeth figured. The secret was out and the damage was done. The task now was to repair it. But how?

Fourteen

"What a fantastic party," Maria complimented Lila that night.

Lila smiled smugly. "Isn't it?"

The evening was getting off to a fabulous start. The back lawn of Fowler Crest had been transformed by the magic of hundreds of Japanese lanterns; the rich, sensuous sound of live jazz wafted on the soft night air. Uniformed waiters circulated among the party guests, carrying silver trays displaying elegant hors d'oeuvres. *No hot dogs and hamburgers on the grill for me!* Lila thought with satisfaction.

"Look, Arthur's here!" Terri announced. "But where's Dana?"

Lila, Amy, and Maria all turned to look. Lila's smile widened. It was the moment she had been waiting for. Forget the music and the food and the decorations. Without a doubt, the highlight of the party in Lila's opinion was the sight of a tuxedoed

Arthur Castillo strolling into the gathering looking indescribably handsome . . . and unmistakably alone. Everything was going to work out perfectly! The party that had threatened to turn into an engagement celebration for Arthur and Dana would now be the setting for a new royal romance.

Arthur's solo entrance caused a buzz of gossip and speculation to sweep through the party. A few reporters, lingering discreetly on the fringes, snapped photos of the prince.

The four girls put their heads close together. "Where's Dana?" Amy asked Lila. "Everybody thought they'd be announcing their engagement tonight. Why do you suppose Arthur didn't bring her?"

Lila shrugged. "I have absolutely no idea," she drawled.

"Maybe she's sick," Terri guessed.

Just then Jessica raced up. "She's not sick," she said in an excited whisper. "Arthur came over to our house this morning to talk to Elizabeth and he was really upset. Right after he left, Liz went over to Dana's. I think they had a fight and Liz was trying to get them back together. But it didn't work!"

Maria's dark eyes grew wide. "You mean they broke up?"

Terri gasped. "But why? They were so happy together!"

"Did Liz say what happened?" asked Amy.

Jessica nodded. "She did. And it turns out— you're not going to believe this . . ."

Amused, Lila listened as Jessica told the others about the tradition of the crown prince's betrothal and the pressure on Arthur to find a bride before

131

he returned to Santa Dora. *It happened just the way I wanted it to!* she exulted. *Dana gave Arthur the boot. She sent him packing. And look where he landed— right at my feet.*

"I want more details. Let's go talk to Elizabeth," Amy suggested.

Amy, Terri, and Maria hurried off, leaving Jessica and Lila alone. "I guess Arthur and Dana have had it," Jessica observed. She squeezed her friend's arm. "What a lucky break for you, Li!"

"Luck had nothing to do with it," Lila informed Jessica.

"What do you mean?"

"How do you suppose Dana found out about the secret tradition?"

"A newspaper reporter told her," Jessica said.

"Well, and how do you suppose the reporter found out?"

"Someone must have leaked the story, and actually Elizabeth thought—" A light dawned in Jessica's eyes. "It was *you?*"

Lila nodded. "I did some research at the library yesterday and then I shared my discovery with Daddy's good friend, the publisher of the *Sweet Valley News.* The rest is history!"

"I'll say. Arthur and Dana sure are, anyway!" Jessica shook her head in disbelief.

"Don't look so scandalized. It's not like I committed a crime. I just made sure Dana found out the truth, which she was bound to do sooner or later. What's wrong with that?"

"I'll tell you what's wrong." Jessica put her hands on her hips. "Liz thought *I'm* the one who told!"

Lila laughed. "Too bad. Well, Jess, I've really got

to be going. Arthur's my guest of honor and I can see he needs my attention desperately. Start getting used to the idea of calling me Your Royal Highness, OK?"

Lila cheerfully turned her back on Jessica's scowl. She spotted Arthur standing with Todd, Ken, Barry, and Winston on the other side of the patio and strolled toward him at a leisurely pace. There was really no rush, she decided. After all, Arthur wasn't going anywhere!

She approached the boys in time to see Winston pat a glum-looking Arthur on the shoulder. "Girls—you can't live with 'em, and you can't live without 'em," Winston commiserated.

"Don't give up," Ken coached the prince. "I bet Dana will come around."

"No, she won't." Arthur's eyes were dark with despair. "It's over."

That was Lila's cue. Arthur was in pain, and Lila knew all about pain. He needed, as she had—still did, even—someone to soothe his wounded pride and broken heart. *And* he needed a new princess!

"Arthur! I'm so glad you could make it. But you haven't had anything to eat or drink!" Taking the prince's arm, Lila steered him away from the others. "I want you to tell me what you think of the punch, and there are some delicious snacks to nibble on—"

"Thanks, Lila, but I'm not really hungry." Arthur stood with his hands in his pockets and his shoulders slumped.

"Well, if you're not hungry, then let's dance." Lila practically dragged Arthur to the temporary parquet dance floor that had been set up on the lawn. Slipping her arms around his waist, she began moving to the music, taking a moment to flash a bright smile at a photographer from the *News*. Arthur shuffled his feet reluctantly. "I'm sorry about what happened with Dana," Lila purred. "She really treated you poorly. Just put her out of your mind."

"I can't do that," Arthur said.

"You could try," Lila urged. "You know, I never thought she was right for you, anyway. You deserve *much* better, Arthur."

Arthur's feet stopped moving abruptly. He shook himself free of Lila's arms. "Excuse me, Lila. Thank you, but I—I have to—" Still stammering his excuses, Arthur left Lila standing alone on the dance floor.

She stared after him, her cheeks flaming. What a low-class cad, to ditch her in the middle of a dance like that, right in front of everybody! *Some prince!* Lila thought, fuming. *Maybe he and Dana deserve each other after all!*

Jessica had known Lila for a long time, but she was pretty sure she had never seen her friend look so foolish. "She threw this whole party just for Arthur, and he doesn't even want to dance with her!" she said gleefully to Sam, Elizabeth, and Todd.

Elizabeth gave Jessica an ironic look. "Gee, who does that remind you of?"

"Lila's much more pathetic than I ever was," Jessica declared. "I mean, I just had a teensy-weensy crush on Arthur." Jessica squeezed Sam's hand. He gave a disgusted snort. "Lila went to a lot of trouble to break up Arthur and Dana so Arthur would go out with her instead."

"So it's Lila's fault Arthur and Dana broke up!" Elizabeth cried.

Jessica nodded. "You were right about her plotting. She's been working on it for *weeks*. Just yesterday she found out Arthur was under pressure from royal tradition to choose a bride on this trip. She read about it at the library and then last night she told the *Sweet Valley News*. She knew Dana would completely blow up over it!"

"And look where it's gotten her," Todd observed. "Nowhere!"

The twins and their boyfriends watched as Lila stomped off the dance floor. Steam was practically coming out of her ears.

"You're right, Todd. Sabotaging Arthur and Dana's relationship hasn't helped Lila's princess campaign one bit." Jessica grinned. "I'd say Arthur wants to marry her about as much as he wants to marry Lady Tracy Windsor!"

"Poor Lila," Sam said. "I feel bad for her."

Elizabeth sighed. "Poor *Arthur*. Maybe I should go talk to him."

"You'd better move fast," Sam advised.

Arthur was walking away across the lawn with Paolo and Justino. There was something very final about his slow but purposeful stride; it left the distinct impression that he wouldn't be coming back. And he had only just arrived!

Jessica looked back at Lila. Even from a distance, it was easy to read her face. The hostess was stunned, insulted, and mortified. It would have been devastating enough if Dana and Arthur had used Lila's bash to announce their engagement. But a party for Prince Arthur, without Prince Arthur . . . how humiliating!

* * *

Elizabeth gazed after Arthur's retreating figure. She hated seeing him look so miserable and defeated. *He came to Sweet Valley to have a good time, to see his old friends and make some new ones. And look what happened!*

It was such a shame. But maybe it didn't have to end this way. Elizabeth reflected on her conversation with Dana that morning. Dana had come across as entirely hard-hearted, but was she, really? *She's always acted tough,* Elizabeth thought. *Hard outside, soft inside. So maybe . . .* "I'll be right back," Elizabeth said to Todd.

Elizabeth ran across the lawn after Arthur. She caught him just as he was about to step into the royal limousine. "Arthur!" she called breathlessly. "Wait a minute!"

Arthur turned. "Elizabeth," he said, his voice flat and dull.

"Can I talk to you?"

Arthur shrugged his assent. They walked a few feet away from the limo. Elizabeth took Arthur's hand. "I just wanted to tell you not to lose hope," she began. "I'd bet anything Dana's not as mad as she's pretending to be. She's just upset—she thinks you wanted to marry her only so you wouldn't have to marry Lady Tracy. Another girl in town who is jealous of Dana made sure Dana found out about the tradition of the crown prince needing to be engaged by his seventeenth birthday. Dana hasn't stopped caring for you, Arthur. Try one more time to explain, and tell her you love her," Elizabeth urged. "She may change her mind."

Arthur smiled bitterly. "Thanks for trying to make me feel better, Elizabeth. But I know Dana.

She's strong-willed and opinionated. She won't change her mind. And she shouldn't!" He clenched his jaw. "These stupid traditions!" he cried. "Royalty is a curse. Dana was right about that—she was right all along. It's ruining my life and it would have ruined hers. She's smart to want no part of it."

"But if you care for each other, maybe—"

Arthur waved off Elizabeth's attempt at consolation. "Dana is too good for me," he said. "She's too good for Santa Dora."

By the light of the Japanese lanterns lining the driveway of Fowler Crest, Elizabeth could see tears glistening in Arthur's eyes. Her own throat tightened with sadness. "No," Arthur concluded, sighing deeply. "Dana will never take me back. And since I can't bear to stay in Sweet Valley another day without her..." He squeezed Elizabeth's hand gently, then released it. "I'm flying back to Santa Dora in the morning, Elizabeth. Goodbye."

The limousine door slammed shut. Justino revved the quiet, powerful engine. As Elizabeth watched the limo drive away she had a feeling she would never see Arthur Castillo again. And neither would Dana.

Fifteen

Dana dropped her mountain bike on the grass. Then she threw herself underneath a tree in her front yard. *That felt so good*, she thought, breathing in big lungfuls of fresh, fragrant air. She had gotten up as the sun was rising, dressed in bike shorts and a big T-shirt, and hit the road, riding ten miles up the coast and ten miles back.

The exercise had been just what she needed to clear her head. Being alone with the huge blue sky, the sea, the hills, and the sun gave Dana a new perspective on things. Her anger had faded, and in its place was a deep regret. All she could think about was how much fun it would have been if Arthur were with her, sailing along the scenic coast road, both of them feeling as free and wild as birds.

We had so many wonderful times. . . . Dana plucked a handful of grass, remembering. Slow-dancing to Lynne's song at Jessica's party; movies, bowling, drives in the limo, walks on the beach; the afternoon on the sailboat, when Arthur kissed her for the first time; La Maison Blanche and the diamond ring; even the debate.

All it took was a little imagination and Dana could remember exactly what it had felt like to have Arthur's arms around her, and to kiss him. She could picture his face, hear his voice. And the boy she pictured wasn't arrogant and selfish and manipulative. He was the crown prince of Santa Dora, yes, but he was also good-hearted, caring, upright, and sincere.

Arthur wasn't just pretending to love me, Dana realized with a sigh. *His feelings were real—as real as mine.* She grimaced, remembering the horrible words she had hurled at him the previous day and the awful way she had treated Elizabeth. What a temper tantrum!

It was hard for Dana to admit that she had been wrong, even to herself. But now that a day and a night had gone by, she could see that she'd really flown off the handle. She had been too quick to judge Arthur. And not only that, she'd judged him on secondhand news—she hadn't even given him a chance to explain his side of the story. *I should probably feel sorry for him,* Dana thought wryly. What a drag, to have to come up with a fiancée by the time you turned seventeen or else get stuck marrying someone you hated!

No doubt about it, Santa Dora really had some absurd traditions. Arthur should have been more open with her—no doubt about that, either. But Dana also knew she could have been more patient and understanding—a lot more.

Suddenly, a feeling of love and hope as warm

as the morning sun flooded Dana's heart. Maybe it didn't have to be over for good between her and Arthur! Could it hurt to give him one more chance? One more chance to explain the situation and convince her that he really loved her?

Thunk. Something landed on the grass next to Dana. She sat up, shielding her eyes against the sun. The paper girl waved to her. Dana waved back.

Reaching over, Dana grabbed the Sunday newspaper and unfolded it. For a moment, she stared at the black-and-white photograph on the front page. It made her sick to her stomach, but she couldn't tear her eyes away.

It was a picture of Arthur and Lila, taken at Lila's party the previous night. They were dancing with their arms around each other; Lila's face was very close to Arthur's and she was smiling smugly.

Dana's breath came fast; all the fury and pain rushed back full force. *Unbelievable! He's going after Lila now!* She threw the paper down in utter disgust. Well, Lila could have him. In Dana's opinion, those two deserved each other!

Elizabeth parked the Jeep on the street in front of the Larsons' house. She had taken a gamble coming over this early; she wasn't sure if anyone would be up yet.

To her relief, she saw Dana sitting in the front yard. Elizabeth walked up the driveway, a friendly smile on her face. "Nice morning for a bike ride," she called.

Dana's own expression was stubbornly unwelcoming. "Hmm," she grunted.

Undeterred, Elizabeth sat down next to Dana.

There wasn't any time to waste. She knew she had to say what she'd come to say, whether Dana was receptive or not. "Dana, Arthur's leaving town this morning because he's so brokenhearted over what happened between the two of you."

"Yeah, right," Dana scoffed. Grabbing the newspaper that was lying nearby, she shoved it under Elizabeth's nose. "He looks pretty sad about the fact that Lila's hanging all over him."

Elizabeth examined the photograph on the front page. "Oh, Dana," she said sorrowfully, "did you really *look* at this picture? Do you really think Arthur was having a good time? He left the party early—I'd say he stayed an hour at most. I'm sure he was dancing with Lila only to be polite. It's not his fault she's the ultimate diehard would-be princess!"

Elizabeth watched Dana's face carefully. Dana took a second look at the picture in the paper, her expression softening somewhat. Elizabeth pressed her point. "He's leaving," she said quietly. "He's going back to Santa Dora today, and he may never come back."

"So? He can go to the moon for all I care," Dana declared proudly.

There was something about Dana's manner—she was *too* defiant, Elizabeth thought. She was hiding her real feelings. "Do you really mean that?" Elizabeth asked.

Dana stared back at Elizabeth. Slowly, her tough facade crumbled. Her eyes filled with tears. "Oh, Liz, I'm just so confused," she cried in frustration. "I don't know how I feel about Arthur anymore. I was in love with him . . . maybe I still am . . . but so many things keep getting in the way! Arthur being a prince and having to live according to all these crazy royal traditions, the constant public scrutiny—how can we ever untangle our relationship from all that? How are we supposed to figure out what we really feel for each other?"

"It's hard," Elizabeth admitted. "But Arthur's trying to do it. I know one thing for a fact, Dana, and it's the last thing I'm going to say on the subject because I've interfered too much already! Custom or no custom, Arthur Castillo loves you. With all his heart." Elizabeth got to her feet. "From here on, it's up to you."

As the Jeep drove off, the simple truth of Elizabeth's words finally registered on Dana. *Arthur's been as confused as I am, but he loves me. He really does love me!*

Just then, the distant sound of an airplane's engines caught Dana's attention. Looking up into the sky, she saw a silver jet high up. Elizabeth had said Arthur was flying home that very morning. Was it too late? Had she thrown away her chance to have one last talk with Arthur, to patch things up, to hug him one last time?

Dana knew it was now or never. Every second counted. She jumped to her feet and then sprinted inside for her car keys. A minute later, she was on the road, racing to Arthur's hotel. *Please let him still be there*, she prayed as she parked the car. *Please don't let him have left yet!*

Elizabeth closed the front door behind her and headed for the kitchen. When she got there she found Jessica in the process of pouring a huge bowl of cereal.

"Careful, Jess," she said teasingly. "You'll put the cereal company out of business."

"Very funny. Two people on my case in one morning. What is this? My lucky day?" Jessica sat down heavily in her chair.

"Sorry. I was just joking. Who's the other annoying person in your life?" Elizabeth asked as she joined her sister at the kitchen table.

Jessica swallowed a spoonful of cereal before answering. "Lila, that's who."

"She called?"

"No." Jessica sighed. "I called her. I was feeling kind of bad for gloating when Arthur left early last night, so I called to apologize. What a mistake!" Jessica dug into her cereal again with gusto.

"I gather she took out all of her anger on you?" Elizabeth asked, pouring herself a cup of coffee from the pot on the table.

"You gathered right." Jessica paused. "Actually, I think her problem is more than anger. I think there's something else going on. She seems *really* bummed about the whole thing. I honestly thought she was only after Arthur for his money and his title." Jessica shrugged. "I mean, you know how Lila is."

Elizabeth frowned. "You mean, I know how Lila *was*. Now that I think about it, I have a feeling that for Lila, getting Arthur to like her meant a lot more than just snagging a rich boyfriend. Don't get me wrong," Elizabeth added. "I still think what she did to Dana was pretty horrible. But I *do* think I'm beginning to understand her motivation."

Jessica stopped chewing and seemed to be considering. "I think I see what you're saying," she said finally. "There were times during Arthur's visit when I thought Lila was losing her mind. All those crazy excursions—"

"What crazy excursions?" Elizabeth interrupted.

Jessica shook her head. "Never mind the details. The point is that she was getting really out of hand, even for Lila. It was like she'd do *anything* to make Arthur notice her."

"I think," Elizabeth said slowly, "that for Lila, Arthur represented a boy totally different from John Pfeifer. John *seemed* like a nice guy, but he wasn't what he appeared to be. Lila probably thought there was less of a risk that Arthur, brought up to be polite and respectful, would turn out to be a creep."

"And he *didn't*," Jessica protested.

"I'm not *saying* he did," Elizabeth agreed. "What I'm saying is that to *Lila*, Arthur's not showing any real interest in her was more than just your average rejection."

Jessica tapped her chin with her spoon. "Poor Lila! Arthur was probably the only guy in Sweet Valley who didn't know about what happened with John Pfeifer."

Elizabeth took a sip of her coffee. "I'm just glad that Lila is still in counseling at Project Youth. It's going to take a while for her life to get back to normal."

"Yeah, I guess you're right, Liz. Lila probably feels pretty abandoned right now. I should call her back." Jessica grinned. "But not before I find out what happened between you and Dana this morning!"

Elizabeth grimaced. "Not much, I'm afraid. And anyway, how did you know I went over to Dana's?"

Jessica rolled her eyes. "Please, Liz! You're always the Wakefield to the rescue!"

"Well, I have a feeling I botched this rescue attempt. I just hope you have more luck with Lila than I had with Dana!"

Breathless, Dana burst into the lobby of the Palm Bay Hotel. And there he was, standing near the counter, surrounded by suitcases, and wearing his royal uniform. *Prince Arthur of Santa Dora*, Dana thought with a rush of emotion, remembering her first sight of him at the airport three weeks earlier.

She stopped, suddenly feeling awkward and shy. Just then, Arthur looked up.

For an instant, he stared at her as if he couldn't quite believe his eyes. Then his whole face brightened. In a few long strides, he was at her side. "Dana!" he exclaimed, his voice hoarse with emotion.

"Hi," she said, her own voice shaky. "I'm—I'm glad I caught you in time. I just wanted to—I think we need to talk."

Arthur nodded. Taking her arm gently, he guided her to a quiet corner of the lobby.

Dana took a deep breath. "I'm sorry I got so mad at you." She smiled wryly. "Or maybe I'm not sorry about that, but I *am* sorry I didn't explain *why* I was mad! I was mad because . . . because I thought you didn't love me. I found out about the tradition and I thought you proposed to me just so your parents couldn't make you marry Lady Tracy."

"That wasn't it at all, Dana." Arthur took both her hands in his and squeezed them tightly. "I was thinking about the tradition, I can't deny it. But

145

even if the tradition didn't exist, I'd still want to marry you."

"I understand why you'd want to keep quiet about it. You have enough girls chasing you as it is! But why didn't you tell *me* about it?" Dana asked.

Arthur shook his head. "I took the custom for granted—it didn't occur to me to mention it. I guess I was so worried about whether you'd even consider becoming a member of my royal family, knowing how you felt about us and our traditions, that I overlooked the possibility of the betrothal tradition itself offending you!"

They held hands and looked at each other. Dana's anger had melted away. "I'm sorry we wasted our last weekend together fighting," she said softly.

"It was all my fault," Arthur said. "But one good thing *did* come from all this."

"What's that?"

"Late last night, I made a decision," he told her. "It's time for me to stand up against this unfair, outdated tradition. I'm not going to announce my betrothal before my seventeenth birthday, and I'm also not going to marry anyone I don't want to."

"But what will your parents say about that?"

"I don't know," Arthur admitted. "I'll talk it over with them as soon as I get back to Santa Dora. Either they will agree with me that it's time to abandon this particular custom, or they will make my younger brother crown prince in my place."

Arthur's determination impressed Dana. "I'm proud of you," she said, her eyes glowing.

He smiled crookedly. "We've really come full aven't we? I learned a lot from you, Dana, starting from the day we had our debate. Falling in love with you taught me that there are times when traditions don't fit with real life. Sometimes you have to question them instead of just mindlessly accepting them. Traditions are valuable, but even more valuable is having the freedom to direct your own destiny. I must marry the person I want when I want. No one should make such an important decision for me."

Arthur wrapped his arms around Dana's shoulders. They hugged each other close. "I'm proud of you. It takes a lot of courage to make changes," Dana said.

"One thing hasn't changed, though," Arthur declared. "I want to ask you a question I asked you once before. But now I'm more serious than ever. I love you, Dana. Will you marry me someday?"

Dana looked up at the prince. With Arthur's arms around her, Dana felt pure happiness. It was so good to have overcome their misunderstandings!

But with their reconciliation had come a new, clearer vision of the situation. "I love you, too," she replied at last. "But I can't commit myself to you now. There's too much I want to do before I settle down. I'm just not ready to be engaged." Disappointment erased the hope in Arthur's eyes. Dana gave him a squeeze. "Besides," she added with a smile, looking down at her bike shorts, hightop sneakers, and wacky T-shirt, "when all is said and done, I'm not the princess type."

Arthur grinned. Then his expression grew serious again. "Don't sell yourself short, Dana," he said. "You are more noble and royal than any girl I've ever known."

From across the lobby, someone called Arthur's name. It was Paolo. "Looks like it's time to go," Dana said, her voice husky.

Arthur nodded. "I'll never forget you, Dana."

"I'll never forget you, either," she promised. "Let's stay close, OK? I mean, as close as we can, considering the fact that we live half a world apart!"

"OK. And who knows?" Arthur managed a smile. "Maybe a few years down the road, we'll be ready to give our relationship another try."

"I'd like that," Dana whispered.

She lifted her face to Arthur's for one last kiss. It was warm and gentle and salty; they were both crying. Finally, Dana pushed Arthur away with a little laugh. "You'd better get moving, Your Royal Highness, or you'll miss your plane!"

Out on the curb, Justino and Paolo had already loaded the bags. The door to the limousine stood open; there was nothing left for Arthur to do but climb inside.

Dana and the prince stood for a moment on the walk in front of the hotel. Finally, Arthur took her hand. Raising it, he placed it gently against his chest. "Goodbye, Princess Dana," he whispered. Then he was gone.

Dana waved after the limo until it disappeared from sight. *Goodbye, Prince Arthur*, she thought.

Suddenly, she wished she could run after the limousine. There was one last thing she would have liked to share with Arthur. She would have liked to tell him that he had taught her something, too—that true royalty was an inner quality, not just a question of a title. By that standard, Dana Arthur Castillo was indeed a real prince.

Sixteen

"Things are so *quiet* around here," Amy complained at lunch on Monday.

"Prince Arthur's gone and we all have to return to our boring everyday lives," Maria agreed with a sigh.

"Even Dana does," said Jessica. "I still can't believe she said no to Arthur's marriage proposal. She could have been princess of Santa Dora! I will *never* understand the way that girl thinks."

"I understand her completely," Lila interjected. "Who'd want to be stuck for the rest of her life with a loser like Arthur, even if he is filthy rich and famous? He's also rude, pompous, self-centered—I could go on, but I don't want to waste my breath."

"Rude, pompous, self-centered . . . hmm." Jessica's eyes twinkled mischievously. "No matter how you look at it, Lila, Prince Arthur's still your perfect match!"

"Put a sock in it," Lila recommended sourly.

"OK. I was only teasing," Jessica said. "Prince Arthur is yesterday's news, anyway. What I'm excited about today are the tryouts for the new play!"

"But it's Shakespeare." Amy wrinkled her nose. "Isn't that stuff kind of heavy for a school play?"

"Yeah, why couldn't they put on a musical, something fun?" wondered Maria.

"Didn't you listen to the announcement at the assembly this morning?" Jessica berated her uncultured friends. "This won't be an ordinary school play. The Goodman Theatre Company is coming to Sweet Valley High to cast and direct the production. We'll get to work with *professionals!*"

"You mean like Brandon Hunter of soap opera fame?" Amy kidded.

"Hardly," Jessica said disdainfully. "These people are the real thing—classically trained Shakespearean actors, people who have reached the pinnacle of dramatic achievement."

"Still, *Macbeth* is *Macbeth*," Maria said. "It sounds a lot like homework to me!"

"Well, sure, if you just *read* it, it sounds like homework," Jessica conceded. "But when it's acted out by someone who's beautiful and talented beyond belief . . ."

"Are you trying to tell us something?" Lila asked.

"Yes," said Jessica. "For your information, you're looking at the future star of the play, Lady Macbeth herself!"

"Lady Macbeth? Isn't she old?" asked Amy.

"*Au contraire!*" Jessica fished around in her ~~shoulder~~ bag for the script. Opening it, she skimmed a ~~page w~~ith relish. "Lady Macbeth is rich, gorgeous, smart, and scheming. She'll do anything to get what she wants, which is to be queen. And men can't resist her. The role is perfect for me."

"Ha," snorted Lila.

Jessica's eyes grew misty. The rave reviews of her performance as Lady Macbeth would draw dozens of talent scouts to the Sweet Valley High auditorium—the play would be her springboard to stardom. *Broadway, here I come!*

She woke from her daydream in time to notice that a girl at the next table was staring at her. The girl caught Jessica's eye and quickly turned away, her pale cheeks flushing.

"Who *is* that mousy, pathetic creature?" Jessica asked her friends in a loud whisper.

"She's new," answered Maria. "Paula somebody."

Paula somebody, a new girl, Jessica reflected, suddenly feeling tolerant. Poor kid—obviously she was just a wannabe, gazing with longing at Jessica and her popular companions.

"Yep, the role is mine for the taking," Jessica declared, closing the script with a flourish in case Paula was still watching.

And the role would be hers; Jessica was sure of it. Maybe she had lost the chance to be a real-life princess, but nothing could stop her from playing royalty on the stage. *And this time, when it comes to casting, I won't have any competition,* Jessica thought with assurance. Because she was going to give the most brilliant audition ever seen at Sweet Valley High!

Jessica Wakefield is determined to get the role of a lifetime—but will she succeed? Find out in Sweet Valley High #92, **SHE'S NOT WHAT SHE SEEMS.**

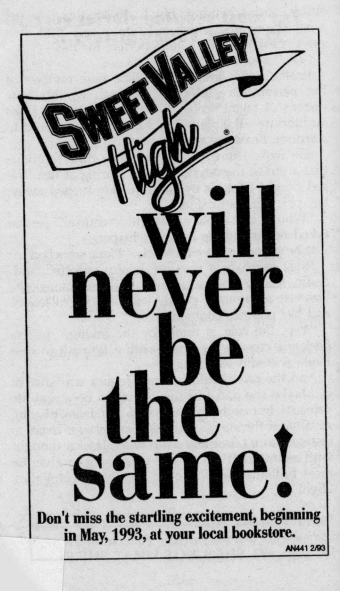

The most exciting stories ever in Sweet Valley history...

FRANCINE PASCAL'S

SWEET VALLEY Saga

☐ **THE WAKEFIELDS OF SWEET VALLEY**
Sweet Valley Saga #1
$3.99/$4.99 in Canada   29278-1
Following the lives, loves and adventures of five
generations of young women who were Elizabeth and
Jessica's ancestors, The Wakefields of Sweet Valley
begins in 1860 when Alice Larson, a 16-year-old
Swedish girl, sails to America.

☐ **THE WAKEFIELD LEGACY: The Untold Story**
Sweet Valley Saga #2
$3.99/$4.99 In Canada   29794-5
Chronicling the lives of Jessica and Elizabeth's
father's ancestors, The Wakefield Legacy begins with
Lord Theodore who crosses the Atlantic and falls in
love with Alice Larson.

SWEET VALLEY HIGH

Celebrate the Seasons
with SWEET VALLEY HIGH
Super Editions

You've been a SWEET VALLEY HIGH fan all along—hanging out with Jessica and Elizabeth and their friends at Sweet Valley High. And now the SWEET VALLEY HIGH *Super Editions* give you more of what you like best—more romance—more excitement—more real-life adventure! Whether you're bicycling up the California Coast in PERFECT SUMMER, dancing at the Sweet Valley Christmas Ball in SPECIAL CHRISTMAS, touring the South of France in SPRING BREAK, catching the rays in a MALIBU SUMMER, or skiing the snowy slopes in WINTER CARNIVAL—you know you're exactly where you want to be—with the gang from SWEET VALLEY HIGH.

SWEET VALLEY HIGH SUPER EDITIONS

☐ **PERFECT SUMMER**
25072-8/$3.50

☐ **MALIBU SUMMER**
26050-2/$3.50

☐ **SPRING BREAK**
25537-1/$3.50

☐ **WINTER CARNIVAL**
26159-2/$2.95

☐ **SPECIAL CHRISTMAS**
25377-8/$3.50

☐ **SPRING FEVER**
26420-6/$3.50
